Familiar Strangers

Familiar Strangers:

Stories from America & The Middle East

by Margaret Kahn

Pearlnote Press

Pacific Grove, California

Surely there is a window from heart to heart:
they are not separate and far from each other.

Mevlâna Jalâluddîn Rumi

Table of Contents

Previous Publication Credits

"Understanding the Enemy," *Iowa Woman* , Spring 1992; reprinted in *Ararat*, Autumn 1992; reprinted in *Iowa Woman: In Celebration of Our First 15 Years*, Fall 1995

"Crossing the Border," *Ararat*, Summer 1987

"Familiar Stranger" was the basis of a play that premiered at the Pear Avenue Theatre in Mountain View, CA 2012

A slightly different version of "Ashura" as "Talking Moharrem Blues," *Pangyrus* 2017

"Feast of Sacrifice," *West*, The Sunday magazine of the *San Jose Mercury News*, July 19, 1987

"Taqseem," *Crab Orchard Review*, 2000

"In the Field," *Kalliope*, Fall/Winter 1986

"Black Seeds," *Ararat* Summer 1995

"The Idle Mill," *Ararat*, Spring 1991

Understanding the Enemy

None of the other mothers had a single black eyebrow, two arches linked like a flying bird, on the ridge of their foreheads. It embarrassed Anahid when she was little that her mother was so indifferent to the rules of feminine beauty. But her mother thought such worries were ridiculous.

"What difference does it make?" she used to say. "I cannot change what God has decreed."

But if God had decreed that there would be no space in the line of hair growing from her mother's brow, he had also decreed that at eighty, Helen Azadkhanian would have the body of a forty-year-old. Anahid studied her mother as they walked up the front steps and into the hall of the church. At forty she had been formidable, the great breasts jutting out in front, the buttocks rearing out from behind. At eighty she looked as if she still had the stamina to survive a major disaster.

Inside the door, her mother turned left and followed a long narrow corridor that led them back behind the sanctuary. Anahid trailed after her. She hadn't been inside the church for years. Not this church. Not any church. She thought they would spot her right away as an unbeliever, someone who didn't belong. But her mother had insisted.

"I know I told you that the women in this church have many stupid ideas which I do not agree with," she said. "But they can cook. I can agree with their cooking."

It was high praise, coming from her mother. Anahid had been hungry when they first talked about it. She wanted to taste homemade pilafs and kebabs. Besides, she was feeling guilty. She often felt bored when her mother talked about her current life --about her Bible study groups and her ice cream socials. Maybe if she experienced it first-hand, she would have more interest, or more compassion anyway.

Faced with the possibility of eating all this food, Anahid was suddenly conscious of her own stomach which felt heavy and convex under her cotton skirt. No longer was she thin little Anahid, racing after Mama, a dozen ladies proffering food. So thin, so thin, they would croon, as if she were a little bird they wanted to fatten.

But they weren't pushing food at her now. Every year she became squarer, her center of gravity sinking lower like her mother. There was more hair on her upper lip. Her eyebrows would have grown together if she'd let them. But she wouldn't let them. She waxed all the hair except the hair on her head. That she cut, like a man's. Her mother was horrified.

"Anni, Anni, how could you?" she cried when she saw it, and Anahid suspected she had made a mistake. But never would she admit it. Especially not to her mother. Later when her mother came out with the long thick dark hair, still only partly grey, shaken out of the bun and fallen down the back of her nightgown, Anahid had turned away so she wouldn't feel envious.

In the church kitchen she watched while her mother's friends --or enemies --she could never remember who was on the current black list --set out their dishes. None of them were close friends. Her mother didn't have close friends, except for a woman she had once worked with at the factory. Several times that woman and her mother had gone to the movies together. But then Vera had gotten divorced. Her mother disapproved of divorce. Besides, Vera wasn't Armenian. Not that her mother trusted her own people. She didn't even trust Anahid. She would never tell her about her finances. She even pretended that certain pieces of jewelry Anahid remembered from her childhood had been lost. Anahid had found them once, hidden in her mother's bureau, and wondered if her mother had forgotten or whether she was afraid Anahid might ask her for them.

Not that it mattered. Anahid had her own gold. She didn't need her mother's jewelry. She didn't need anything from her mother. She told herself that a lot lately as a reminder to let her mother be, to appreciate her as she was, to see her through the eyes of others. People were interested in survivors these days. Tell us about the marches. Tell us about the village and what the Turks did, they would say. What did it matter if this passed for history? It made her mother feel important. That was enough. She told herself that she shouldn't be so academic. Everything of value wasn't collected or analyzed in a university. Still, the people making these recordings weren't getting the whole picture. Survivors like her mother couldn't see the whole picture. Every time one of them told their story, something would be left out. No matter how carefully they fit the pieces together, they would never be able to see exactly what it looked like. How could they? They never saw anything but their own side.

One by one her mother introduced her to the other women. Anahid smiled pleasantly and put out her hand. Several of the women leaned forward to kiss her first on one cheek and then the other, in the Middle Eastern style. Her mother frowned slightly when this happened, but Anahid enjoyed it. She had always wished her mother would be like this. Warm, even a little sloppy. Not needing to know someone well or even love them to show physical affection.

"How long are you visiting?" a woman named Mrs. Manoogian asked her.

"Just a few days."

The woman shook her head. "You young people lead such busy lives. I suppose it's a wonder you come to see your old parents at all."

Anahid nodded slightly and then glanced around for her mother. She was trying to make room for her dish in the oven. She wanted to make sure it was exactly the right temperature. Anahid felt awkward watching her. Why couldn't they just sit down and eat? Why did there have to be this endless jockeying and preparation? It reminded her of family dinners and celebrations. Nothing was spontaneous. Everything had to be planned and cooked for days.

She went out into the hall where, amidst the sea of aging females, she spotted a male face, and relatively young. He looked to be in his thirties and not with anyone else. Not a likely candidate for a Wednesday night church supper. She kept glancing at him when she thought he wasn't watching. He wasn't bad looking, if a little too short and well-groomed. Anahid had never been attracted to Armenian men. There was something too fastidious about most of them. Something too careful.

"Excuse me," he said. "Didn't I see you on television the other night'?"

Anahid glanced back, thinking he must be talking about her mother. She was sometimes on the local cable channel talking about the genocide. But her mother was still in the kitchen.

He came closer and put out his hand. "John Hagopian. I teach soil science at U.C. Davis."

Unwillingly, Anahid looked into a pair of warm, but curious brown eyes.

"I didn't expect to run into you at an Armenian church supper. Don't you teach at--?"

Anahid nodded. "I'm on the West Coast to give a talk at Berkeley. "And," she added slowly. "To see my mother."

He grinned. "My mother lives in Massachusetts. In Belmont, they have the same kinds of church suppers."

Anahid felt relieved. Here was someone who knew who she was. Someone to whom she wouldn't have to pretend.

"Shall we sit down?" she asked, deliberately not waiting for her mother.

"Why not?" He smiled and pulled out a chair for her.

Anahid sat down, wondering if she might not be attracted to Armenians after all. Certainly she had missed Arthur less on this trip than any other trip to date. Maybe it had to do with her sudden fame. Not that she really was famous, but people interested in Turks were finally beginning to look to her as an expert. About time, considering all the work she had done.

"Mind if I ask you a question'?"

Anahid nodded.

"How does your mother feel about the field you've chosen?"

Anahid started to choke on her dolma. Hastily, she put her fork down.

John leaned over and pounded her on the back. "I shouldn't have asked such a probing question while you were in the middle of chewing!"

She waved her hand. "No, no, it's OK. It's just that --" She broke off to take a sip of water. "My mother and I don't get along that well, but it's not because I'm in Turkic studies."

He raised his eyebrows.

Anahid explained, "She would have liked to be a scholar herself. She has an analytical cast of mind."

"You mean she is smart?" He narrowed his eyes.

"Yes," Anahid said. "But of course brains weren't the point, were they, back in those days? I mean, not for girls."

He gave a little laugh. "So Turkish culture isn't sexist? Maybe even more sexist than our own?"

Anahid sighed inwardly. The old Christian men's argument. She decided to turn the question back on him. "What about you? How does your mother feel about your field?"

John laughed. "I think she would rather I was in something a little less down to earth than soil science."

"Like what? Turkic studies'?" Anahid suggested and felt relieved when he laughed with her.

They were on their second helpings when her mother appeared. "Anahid, I was looking everywhere for you."Her mother glanced curiously toward John and then away. John pushed back his chair and stood up.

"Please, Mrs. Azadkhanian, I am John--John Hagopian. I recognized your daughter from the film on PBS the other night about the wives of Turks who've settled in Germany."

Anahid glanced quickly at her mother to see if any of this had registered. But her mother was too busy taking food off her tray. Anahid stared at her own plate and sighed.

"You are a member of this church?" her mother asked.

John paused in his eating and shook his head. "No. I teach at Davis."

Her mother narrowed her eyes. "You are married?"

He seemed to be suppressing a smile as he shook his head.

Anahid saw her look pointedly around the room. "I'm sure if you join this church you will find many nice girls."

John nodded and went back to his salad, smiling to himself as if this were a private joke which he alone could appreciate.

Anahid wondered if he could be gay. A gay Armenian. That wasn't something you heard about much. Or maybe he had a live-in lover-- one who didn't relish Armenian church suppers the way he did.

Anahid's gaze swept down the long table. Many forks were being raised and grains of rice were falling through the tines. Food. The great unifying factor. Even now it was the only thing she and her mother could agree on.

"My mother makes khataif too," John was saying.

Anahid looked over at the food table. Should she go and get some dessert? It would be hard to stop at one.

"Where was your mother born?" she heard her mother asking John.

He told her the answer, but Anahid didn't take it in. She was too busy watching the attentive way he leaned toward her. An absurd thought crossed her mind. Maybe he had some kind of penchant for old women.

She stood up and went to the dessert table. Six kinds of baklava. Two kinds of khataif. Chocolate torte. She helped herself to the baklava. One of the women she'd been introduced to earlier appeared at her elbow.

"Try that one. I made it myself. See if you can guess the flavorings."

Anahid set her paper plate down on the edge of the table and laboriously used the plastic fork to cut herself a bite.

"Orange blossom and cardamom," she announced as soon as she'd finished swallowing. "But a little too much sugar. At least for me."

The woman regarded her. "You are your mother's daughter, aren't you?"

Anahid watched as the woman walked away.

Her mother was famous for her accuracy, for her willingness to speak the truth even when the truth wasn't what was wanted or needed. At family gatherings, the ones Anahid could remember, she always pictured her mother off to the side, outside the circle, not saying much until the end when suddenly she would slice into the heart of what everyone else had been trying to avoid.

Anahid pulled out the metal folding chair. John looked up. "Your mother really has a lot of interesting stories."

People were always telling her that. Sometimes she wondered if these people knew what it would be like to live with those stories. Day after day. Year after year. The story of how her mother's little brother died on the march. The story of how her mother came across her own mother's corpse floating in the river. When she was still a little girl, her mother had talked about clutching the body, wanting to hold onto any part of her, rather than live without her.

Anahid thought other children grew up with mothers like this until she went away to college. Other girls' mothers might be crazy and problematic, but they did not tell stories like that. Nor did they deliver their genocide stories in a monotone that made them seem even more horrible. There was something dead about her mother. Anahid had realized this years ago when she and her mother had had a fight-- a big screaming argument. She had run out of the house, tears streaming. She didn't see where she was going until she hit bark. Then she looked up. It was the old elm, one that was dying. The leaves were so far away. All she could touch was the dead part-- the wood.

Anahid remembered coming home from school and waving things in her mother's face. Incessantly talking of people and events while her mother stood at the sink working, always working, without showing any interest. After awhile Anahid had given up. Gone outside. Searched for friends to play with, anyone whose face was not dead.

Anahid studied her now as she spoke to John. She was struck by how animated she was. Her eyes opened wide and then narrowed. She waved her hands around. After awhile Anahid realized it was not a back and forth. Her mother was putting up a screen of words to keep him from getting closer. Whatever would keep him at bay. Maybe that's why her mother resented her so much. Because Anahid, from her very conception, was too close. Her mother couldn't stand to be too close. Anahid had known this from the time she was little. Her mother would turn away from lines or from crowded places, saying they would go another day when it wasn't so busy.

Her father said she should try to understand what her mother had been through and forgive her. But Anahid had been too young. She could imagine surviving. She was young and strong the way her mother had been. She just couldn't imagine the marks such survival left on a person. Now she understood more. She had read enough about it. She had even gone to those places where her mother's heart had figuratively been cut out of her and lost.

"You must be very proud," she suddenly heard John saying. "To have a daughter like Anahid."

Anahid looked up from her desserts. Her mother was grimacing. "Oh yes, well," her mother was saying, as if she wasn't proud at all but just trying to stop herself from saying something she shouldn't. "Anahid has been lucky."

"You know," John leaned forward slightly, almost as if he were about to reveal a secret. "I have a good friend who's a Turk. He loves Armenian cooking. I thought of inviting him here tonight."

Anahid's mother raised her eyebrows, or rather her single eyebrow. Anahid felt like laughing. Poor John. He was probably losing every single point he'd built up in her mother's estimation.

But he didn't seem aware of that. "My friend isn't like this, but many Turks – even educated ones -- still think either there was no massacre or that the Armenians brought it on themselves." He paused and then went on. "Of course we know what we Armenians think of Turks. I think it takes a lot of courage to bridge the gap. To try to understand your own enemy."

Her mother had stopped chewing. John Hagopian went on as if he made these speeches regularly. "One thing that really impressed me was the compassion in your daughter's film. I felt as if she really understood those women and felt for them. When I saw the credits at the end, I was amazed to see an Armenian name."

He went on talking about the film, almost as if he'd memorized it. Anahid wanted to listen but she couldn't take her eyes off her mother. For forty years nothing Anahid could say had penetrated, and now here was John Hagopian, this soil scientist, making her mother pay attention.

"Have you seen Anahid's film?" The question, sprung at the end of all his remarks, caught her mother off guard.

"I wanted to see it," her mother said, glancing away from them, "But I had a meeting I needed to attend."

"You should get someone to copy it for you," he said. "There are going to be reruns."

Her mother nodded docilely. "Yes," she said, looking over at Anahid. "You give me copy, eh Anni?"

Anahid nodded, wondering if this was the beginning of a new era.

Then her mother excused herself. Anahid stared at the broad back shuffling off in the direction of the ladies room. She turned back to John. "Well, that was quite a validation. I'm not sure she could take it all in."

He laughed. "Sorry. Sometimes I get a little carried away."

She smiled at him without saying anything. She was waiting for him to reveal his reason for taking such a personal interest in her situation.

But all he said was, "I hate to see parents not valuing their children."

She nodded.

He went on. "You know it's hard for us to understand what people like your mother lived through. It was like an avalanche of hatred and revenge and murder. Straight out of the blue."

She gazed at him, her appreciation suddenly cooling. "You think so?"

He turned it back on her. "What's your take on it?"

"Sometimes I think, in my heart of hearts, that they brought it on themselves. At least partially. They shouldn't have brought the Russians in as their allies."

"They?" His voice was suddenly hard, and she was surprised to see the features that looked so civilized and refined a moment ago look so threatening.

"I'm not a survivor, the way she is." Anahid said quickly, the old defensiveness rising. "I don't blame every bad thing in my life on the Turks."

"No," he said slowly. "The Turks didn't do anything to you." He paused and narrowed his eyes so that instead of the warm, sympathetic pools they had been when he spoke to her mother, they were narrowed slits.

"Who is your enemy'?" he asked.

She felt startled. "My enemy?"

"Everyone has an enemy. Something they blame for the ills of their life."

She narrowed her own eyes. Why should she confess her sins when he hadn't even said what he was doing here?

He wiped his hands and mouth carefully on a napkin. "I'm afraid I have to be going. It was a pleasure to meet you. I didn't expect such a pleasure when I came here this evening."

He stood up and walked in his careful way across the fellowship hall. Anahid stared after him, wondering why she felt so unsettled. Usually she was the interviewer, the one who asked all the questions.

Her mother came back and sat down heavily. Then she looked all around. "Has he left already?"

"He had a date," Anahid told her.

"A date?" Her mother's forehead wrinkled. "He didn't look like someone who would have a date."

Anahid studied the old leathery face and the burning, skeptical eyes. Was it possible her mother was finally catching on to things? Did she realize that even in this community there could be unattached men who weren't interested in women?

Then her mother spoiled it all by saying, "I think he came to this dinner to try to find someone. Too bad he picked the wrong woman."

For a moment Anahid felt herself being pulled back into the maelstrom. What was too bad, she thought bitterly. The fact that she was already married or the fact that she was Anahid?

"Mama," she said softly.

Her mother leaned toward her, eyes blank to the hurt she had caused.

Anahid paused, forgetting what she had been about to say. "I liked your kibbee," she offered, suddenly remembering what she had meant to say when John was there. "It was delicious."

Her mother waved her hand. "It wasn't my best. You should come another time, when I have time to make it perfectly."

Anahid laid her hand on the firm old thigh. "I'll come another time, but only if you promise to make everything perfect."

Her mother gave her a startled look. Then she saw Anahid was joking. She smiled. A creakingly distrustful sort of smile, but a smile nonetheless. "I make perfect kibbee. You make perfect video on Turks."

"You want to see it?" Anahid asked, her eyes suddenly filling with tears.

"Of course," said her mother, as if there had never been any question.

Had there? Suddenly Anahid didn't know why she had been so sure her mother was always against her.

She waited in a corner of the kitchen, feeling like a small girl again while her mother gathered up her pot, her spatula, and her serving plate.

"Did you like our food?" Another heavy-set church woman came up and poked Anahid playfully in the ribs. "Looks like you ate enough."

Anahid laughed. "I'm getting fat."

"It's OK," the woman said. "Fat is good."

Her mother preceded her. Anahid followed, still unsure of which way to go in the labyrinth of corridors. Then they were outside again, under the stars.

"So, when are you going to show me the videotape of your film, Anni?"

Anahid unlocked her mother's door first. "You wouldn't like it," she said before she went around to the driver's side.

"How do you know I don't like it?" Her mother's English, even after forty years, was still heavy with accent.

"It's about Turks." Anahid inserted the key in the ignition.

"So they happen to be Turks. Do you think I have no forgiveness in me? Anahid, I pray all my life for forgiveness. I am a Christian."

Anahid was silent. She'd heard this before. Mama, I have never seen you forgive anyone. But she couldn't say it out loud.

"I forgive my sister," her mother was going on. "Even after all those terrible things she did to me."

Anahid didn't say anything.

"I even forgive the man who killed my little brother."

Anahid could bear it no more. "I don't believe that, Mama. You didn't forgive any of us. Not even me."

"You? What do I have to forgive you for?" The old face turned toward her. The single eyebrow seemed to be quivering.

Anahid felt afraid. But she couldn't back off now. "For having an easier time than you did. For not having to go on the marches."

Her mother was silent. For a moment Anahid felt terrified. Her mother looked healthy enough but who knew what the heart muscle looked like under that seemingly robust chest.

She drove on, remembering what she used to tell people when she was little. How she wished she had been there during the massacres. People told her she was crazy. It was the luckiest thing in the world

she'd been born in America. She didn't know her own good fortune.
But they didn't know her mother.

It was like walking along a river. One that had no bridges, no
fordable spots, no ferries. Her mother was on one side, and she was on
the other. She glanced over and saw that her mother's mouth was open,
and the burning eyes were shut under that one fierce eyebrow. She put
out her hand, as if she would touch her mother's hair. Then she let her
arm fall. Her mother was leaning away from her, against the window--
as always-- on the far shore.

Daya Habeeba

For several days now Daya Habeeba had been following her around. Wherever she went, Barbara could hear the old woman's blocked breathing passages. She felt the skin on her neck prickle as her mother-in-law without a word, wheezing and sniffling, started some unnecessary task or other while Barbara rushed around trying to tidy up before she left.

Right now she was in the middle of unloading the dishwasher when Daya Habeeba wordlessly sidled up next to her. The odors of saffron and rosewater, sour milk and urine, rose from the skirts of the old woman as she leaned over the sink to run scalding hot water for a second into a single delicate gold rimmed glass. As soon as she'd rinsed it, the glass went straight into the rack. Barbara tried to suppress her irritation. After all Daya Habeeba was the only one who drank from these glasses. They didn't need soap, and probably Daya Habeeba was right when she said they wouldn't survive the dishwasher.

She's just an old woman, Barbara thought, as she went upstairs to get ready for her shift. Not only that, she'd lived through harder times than most Californians could imagine. But these were only platitudes.

As Barbara pulled her nursing uniform out of the closet she reminded herself of how much she had admired this woman before she'd come to live with them. If only she could re-capture the compassion she'd felt!

Instead, a hundred petty concerns filled her mind. She reminded herself to speak to Daya about the figs rotting in her room. Even Aisha commented, holding her little nose and making a face. But Daya, who persisted in gathering up all the half-rotted fruit from the front yard and storing them in her room fought back when Barbara tried to removed the bowls.

"I make vinegar," she insisted. Or even, "syrup."

Simail couldn't be bothered with these squabbles, as he termed them. He was too busy handling cases at the ER to help Barbara manage his mother. He didn't even want to make sure she had her annual physical, something Daya refused to do without her exalted son to take her there.

How long, Barbara wanted to know, since his mother had had her breasts examined. Simail looked at her as if she were crazy. "Kurdish women don't get breast cancer," he finally told her.

"That's because most of them die before it's diagnosed," she'd snapped back.

Now, as she bent over to lace up her comfortable white shoes, Barbara thought about how she had brought this on herself. Simail had been in no rush to invite his mother to live with them.

Just the opposite, in fact. When the Gulf War had ended, messily, for those caught in the mountains between Iran, Iraq, and Turkey, it had been Soreyya, Simail's sister who had taken their mother in.

Soreyya was a doctor as well and busier than Simail with her twins and her dermatology practice, but she was a daughter, not a son with a

British wife. The youngest sister was still in school. The brothers all had foreign wives too. Barbara wondered if they had suggested, as she had, that his mother come and stay with them.

Simail was tight-lipped. "My mother has many requirements," was all he revealed at the time after the family meeting to which she was not invited.

Barbara had only met Daya once before she and Simail had married. That was back in the refugee camp in Iran and only a month or so after she and Simail had themselves met. Simail had come from California to tend to the victims of Saddam Hussein's chemical rain. Barbara had come from closer, the National Health Service in the UK. It was her second foray into disaster relief medicine, and she had loved being in the mountains. Simail had brought a woman with blue eyes gleaming like gemstones in her sun-leathered face to meet the young British he had already decided to take as his wife.

"Barbara, I want you to meet my mother. Daya Habeeba."

Daya's grip had been as strong as a man's, but her voice was already wheezy and cracked from smoking too many cigarettes. Barbara could not have imagined then that she would one day be living in California, and this woman would be her mother-in-law.

She straightened up from tying her shoes and glanced at the alarm clock on the dresser top. She was working four hours a day now at the clinic as a nurse practitioner. Simail didn't want her to work. He said he made enough money as an ER doctor for her to stay home with Aisha. But Barbara needed her independence. She needed also to get away from Daya Habeeba.

As she came down the stairs, she picked up one of Aisha's many stuffed toys and set it at the bottom on top of the banister post. Daya stood next to the last step with a disgruntled look on her face.

"I bring Aisha," she said in her rudimentary English. "Four o'clock," she added, pointing to the clock on the wall.

'Thank you," Barbara said the way she had learned from listening to Simail and his family. "Thank you," like that always meant "no."

But Daya Habeeba was crafty. She understood that "Thank you" in English meant "yes."

"Good," she said, turning away.

"We can go together then," Barbara said, trying to be polite.

When Daya Habeeba first came to live with them, Barbara had taken all her offers at face value. Aisha's daycare was only a few blocks away. For two weeks they had walked this route together. Then Daya had insisted she could do it on her own.

Barbara understood this as Daya's desire to have one-on-one time with Aisha. Or even to make it possible for Barbara to get other work done. But when Daya had failed to follow through on two separate occasions, Barbara no longer took Daya at her word.

She always had excuses, of course. She had taken a nap one day. On another, her knee had hurt. When Barbara said they could go together or that she would pick up her daughter on her own, Daya had taken it as a slap in the face.

Simail, when presented with this, said, "Why do you expect my mother to do anything for you? In Kurdistan, mothers-in-law are queens. Daughters-in-law are their slaves. Remember! It was your idea to bring her here."

The reality of mothers-in-law and their powers back in the old country explained a lot. If only she had known sooner! Unfortunately it was too late to help. The cycle of misunderstanding and hurt had already begun.

Now she said to her mother-in-law in English, "I must pick Aisha up and then run some errands. We will be home later."

The old woman's face fell. Then she brightened. "Not worry. I make dinner."

Once more Barbara had to decline. When the old woman cooked, she left the kitchen in a total mess. The truth was, the food she made didn't taste that good. She had lots of excuses for this too, such as not having the right ingredients.

Barbara said firmly, "Thank you for this offer, Daya Habeeba, but that won't be necessary. Simail's not coming home. I thought I'd pick something up."

"At Chinese restaurant?" There was a quaver in Daya Habeeba's voice.

Barbara hesitated. Daya Habeeba wouldn't eat Chinese food. She would push it around the plate, inspecting the meat. It didn't matter how many times Barbara told her it was chicken or beef, the old woman was still afraid of eating pork, or something worse. On days when Barbara had more time and sympathy she would go to the Iranian place and order a separate dinner, but today she felt too tired and stressed out to make a whole separate trip.

"There are leftovers in the refrigerator," she pointed out.

She saw how the woman's face turned dark, but she had made up her mind. "I'll get a couple of vegetable dishes," she promised. "You won't have to worry what kind of meat is in them." Then she opened the front door.

The man across the way in the circle failed to look up from sweeping the walk. Before Daya Habeeba's arrival, most of the neighbors waved pleasantly and went on about their business. But now they either looked away or aimed pointed stares. They had probably never seen anyone remotely resembling Daya Habeeba. Barbara herself was sometimes startled when she pulled up in front of the house and saw her mother-in-law bending over to gather up rotting figs or wheeling up a grocery cart filled with half a dozen items from the nearby Safeway. She always dressed in the same style -- her hennaed hair bundled in a kerchief, her skirts long and full, the metallic threads glittering in what must have seemed to these suburban Californians like gypsy gaudiness.

Daya Habeeba had a high profile here. Even before arriving in the cul de sac, she had appeared on the evening news. This was before the family had decided who would take her in. She had been staying at Soreyya's house, getting angrier and angrier.

Then, suddenly, there she was on the local evening news! Wearing her two dresses, one over the other, the gauzy scarf wound tight around her head, a cardboard sign, crudely lettered in English.

"Kurd refugee lady. No home. Please help."

The back story came out quickly, not over network television, but via the phone lines. The situation between her and her eldest daughter Soreyya had been deteriorating for weeks. The two of them weren't speaking. Daya Habeeba had locked the door to her room.

That afternoon she had mysteriously disappeared only to appear again on the evening news.

"Local fallout from the Gulf War," had been the headline.

The call from the county social worker came quickly. She was terribly sorry, but she needed to investigate a charge of possible elder abuse. The siblings complained, especially the brothers, about how impossible Soreyya was. Just like their mother in fact.

Barbara sat listening that night as they traded stories in her living room of their mother's escapades – how she had pushed an Iraqi soldier who was threatening Simail once, how she had kicked their father out of the house after he had taken a second wife, how she had crossed the border into Turkey after one of the wars, alone and with no one to guide her past the mines.

"You should be the one who takes her," Soreyya had said to Simail.

"And why is that?"

"Because you are her favorite."

Simail had laughed. "Definitely a mixed blessing," he'd said, throwing a glance at Barbara.

That night she had made her pitch. "Why don't we?"

"It's for your sake I decline," he told her.

Barbara thought of her own mother, a heavy smoker dead of a heart attack in Manchester at the age 38.

"She's got nowhere else."

So Daya Habeeba had arrived on their doorstep, her worldly possessions around her in paper shopping bags.

"Welcome," Barbara had said in her rudimentary Kurdish.

She had thought the old woman would at least smile at her, but she was still too angry about what had happened at Soreyya's house and the way the social worker had let her down. Barbara gave up her sewing room. "Here is your room," she said, opening the door to what she felt was the best room in the house – with the view of the white oak -- tucked under the eaves, away at the end of the hall so that it was almost in a little world of its own.

"So small," Daya Habeeba had muttered under her breath in Kurdish as if Barbara couldn't understand.

One day she came home and found Daya Habeeba rifling through her dresser drawers. The old woman didn't even blush.

"I look for more soap," she'd said disingenuously although they both knew perfectly well it wasn't there.

More than anything Barbara wanted not to have this feeling of dissatisfaction in her house. She hated seeing the permanent scowl on Daya Habeeba's face and the corresponding blankness it evoked in Simail. As for Aisha, she had reverted to sucking her thumb.

Barbara pulled into the hospital parking lot and then checked her own face. She could see permanent frown lines developing between her eyebrows. She remembered one of the reasons Simail had given for wanting to marry her.

"I want a woman who knows how to be happy," he'd said.

Barbara was thinking about all this as she pulled back into the driveway. Night had fallen, and Aisha was sucking her thumb in the back seat. The house was dark. She hurried inside, holding the bag of Chinese takeout.

Aisha went past her. "Dapeer not here," she called out.

Barbara felt exhausted. They sat at the table. The two of them were starving. First they would get some food inside them and then deal with Daya Habeeba.

"I don't understand. When did you last see her?" Simail was leaning over the table, his hair hanging across his forehead.

"Your mother was gone by the time we came back with the takeout."

Simail pressed his lips together under his mustache.

Barbara stared at him. She understood better now how Soreyya had felt when the rest of the family had turned their anger on her.

"I've been driving around for hours," she said. "I looked everywhere she might conceivably have gone."

Simail shook his head. "I knew we shouldn't have taken her in."

She thought of all the things she could say, but she instead she stayed silent. That was her way – the way she'd been brought up, not to cry out when she was hurt, not to argue for herself.

Simail's gaze was cold. "Have you called Soreyya?"

It was one of those moments when she knew that no matter how many years they were married she would always be the outsider. Wordlessly she passed him the phone. Then she went upstairs and stood in the doorway, staring at what used to be her refuge. Daya Habeeba saved everything – bottles she found on walks around the neighborhood, letters she carried around with her, old newspapers, bags from stores, and of course the infamous rotting figs.

Barbara squatted down and picked up the bowl. The fermented smell made her think of the yogurt back in Iran. It didn't smell or taste like American yogurt with its simple sour flavor. Iranian yogurt had picked up the smell of time itself, as many foods there had, by sitting for much longer periods without stabilizing chemicals, without antiseptic bowls, absorbing the microbes of the bazaar.

The smell brought it back to her – how she had felt when she first met Simail, how brave she thought his mother was, and her own desire to save them – not just mother and son, but all of them. When she was in the camps she had been in awe of the hospitality people managed to show. She didn't know how they did it. She would sit in tent after tent and be offered tea and seeds and feel as if she were visiting royalty. Surely in her own house, she could have matched that. But it turned out she couldn't.

Downstairs in the kitchen, she ran scalding water into the bowl that had held the figs. Then she glanced over at the rack and saw the lone tea glass. The gold rim gleamed along with the gold leaf birds. Daya Habeeba had brought these glasses as a present, but neither Barbara nor Simail had wanted to use them. Simail drank only coffee and Barbara, who loved tea, hadn't wanted to use them once she realized they wouldn't go through the dishwasher. Daya Habeeba had tried to share them with Aisha who had dropped one and shattered it. After that, she used them alone. Barbara picked up the finjan and put it carefully back in the cabinet with the rest of the set.

The days passed. They contacted the police who had no clue as to what might have happened.

"She is that gypsy-looking woman who appeared on the evening news saying she was homeless?" one officer asked in a bemused voice.

Then a woman teaching Kurdish at the University of California contacted them. This woman had come to visit Daya Habeeba shortly after she had appeared on the evening news. It was just after Daya Habeeba had come to live with them. Habeeba had pulled out all of her treasures – the necklaces she had made using bits of wood and Iraqi coins, the crumbling book of Kurdish poetry, some ancient pictures of her family. The woman had acted interested. She'd given Daya Habeeba her card. But she had never come to visit again, and Daya Habeeba had hesitated to call.

"She not speak my language," she said.

Barbara didn't understand this. Carolyn taught Kurdish. Simail had explained that Carolyn, the scholar, spoke southern Kurdish while his mother spoke northern.

Now Carolyn was saying, "I got a fax from this import-export company in Turkey. I had no idea who sent it. It came in over the departmental fax machine. They weren't sure who it was for. They gave it to the Turkish teacher first who gave it to me. She recognized the word, "Daya" as being mother in Kurdish."

Barbara felt at a loss. Simail was at the hospital. "Perhaps I could come and pick it up," she said.

"Of course," said Carolyn, sounding relieved.

The fax turned out to be only the beginning. There were more faxes and then phone calls from people who were clearly perplexed. More information came out. Zahra, Simail's youngest sister, had driven Daya to the airport after putting her up for the night in her dorm room

"You all talk so bad about her," the sister said. "You treat her like she's crazy or something." Zahra was the most Americanized of the bunch and the most critical of how they acted. Invariably she took Daya's side in things. Tellingly, she had never been faced with the responsibility of actually taking care of her grandmother for any length of time.

"My mother is playing one of her little power games," Simail said darkly after he found out that Daya had hit people up in her ex-husband's office for a ticket to fly to Turkey on the pretext that she desperately needed to see him. Something was wrong with their son Simail that she needed to discuss with him in person.

Barbara wasn't sure what to do. Some days she considered taking a vacation, just to get away from the oppressive atmosphere. Other days she marveled at the ability of her mother-in-law, an illiterate sixty-something tribal woman, to make trouble for her children. But mostly she watched her husband.

Finally Simail made up his mind. He would take time off to go to Turkey and fetch her. But before he could even start making inquiries, his father called.

Barbara listened to the stiff sound of Simail's voice. At first there were only monosyllables. But then there was more.

When he hung up he said, "I'm not going."

Barbara gazed at him quizzically. Simail's face was grim. "She wants our attention, but she doesn't want our help. When she asks, we'll give it."

She looked into his eyes and remembered the doctor she had met in the camp. The idealist who had said he would never forget where he had come from or the duty he had to help the ones who couldn't escape.

She said, "I'm sorry."

His face sagged, and for a moment she imagined he would cry. "No," he said firmly. "It's my fault."

"How?"

"I should have brought her here earlier when there was still time."

"Time for what?" she wanted to know.

"For her to learn the language. To change her life."

"For some people it's too late the moment they're born."

"You sound like a Middle Easterner," he said.

When Daya Habeeba finally returned it was through no effort of theirs. The Iranians stopped her at the border and wouldn't let her in, even though she had a passport from their government.

"You must send us money to return her to the United States," the customs official told Simail over the phone. He also let him know what he thought of sons who didn't care for their aging mothers properly.

Simail let it go. A few days later Barbara drove to the airport with Aisha in the back seat.

"Dapeer," Aisha called out as Daya Habeeba rolled toward them.

Barbara almost didn't recognize her. The old woman slumped in the wheelchair gazed dully up at them, as if she wasn't sure who they were. "Simail couldn't come," Barbara said. "He had to be at the hospital."

Daya Habeeba didn't respond.

Barbara held on tightly to Aisha's hand as they made their way down the long passageways linking the arrival gates to the parking garage. When they were almost out of the terminal, a man in a uniform came running toward them.

"Stop!" he called out.

Barbara wondered if it would be some new surprise. Perhaps Daya Habeeba was wanted for smuggling. Perhaps this was a customs official realizing his mistake.

"You must surrender wheelchair," he ordered. "It is property of," and then he uttered the Turkish words for the name of the airline.

Barbara glanced at her mother-in-law. She still wasn't saying anything, but her look had changed. The old blue fire blazed up in her eyes.

Barbara wanted to ask what she was supposed to do – carry the old woman to the car? But she had the feeling this airline employee would not be concerned about that. She thought of the stories Simail had told her about how the Turkish government had tried to squash the Kurds' demands for human rights. How Turkish army officers had said in the 1930's that Kurds weren't worth the cost of a bullet so they ran bayonets through their bodies. How even in the 1990's, they were still being systemically tortured and murdered.

She curled her fingers tightly around the top of the wheelchair. "I'm sorry but my mother-in-law needs it."

The official didn't even look at Daya Habeeba. "Come with me back to office, You can call for replacement," he ordered.

Barbara hesitated. Then, without warning, she tightened her grip on Aisha's hand. It was awkward pushing the wheelchair with one hand, but the elevator was only a few feet away. Barbara went toward it. The elevator doors closed in front of the startled official's face. When they reached the level where her car was parked, Barbara pushed Daya Habeeba quickly out and threaded her way between the cars. Miraculously, Aisha kept up.

When they reached the van, Barbara started planning how best to lift the old woman so as not to injure either of them. But when she had the door open, Daya Habeeba calmly climbed out of the chair and up into the front seat.

"I OK," she said, gold teeth gleaming.

Barbara gazed at the chair, which had started to roll backwards.

Daya Habeeba's gaze followed it. "Not worry," she said. "They find chair, later."

Barbara hesitated, wondering if she should go after it. Maybe the airline would call and try to charge them for it. She got into the car. Her mother-in-law was twisted around in her seat babbling away to Aisha about the things she had brought for her.

By the time she got out to the freeway Barbara had stopped expecting to see flashing lights behind her. Instead she was listening to the sound of her daughter imitating her mother-in-law's accent from the back seat.

"Baba says you fight soldier back in Iraq," her daughter was saying.

"He say that?" Daya Habeeba asked in her hoarse smoker's voice.

"Mummy put finjans out on table for tea when you get home."

"I bring something for you too," Habeeba said, patting Barbara's knee.

Barbara glanced at the black headscarf and the old beaked nose. Simail had talked a lot about his mother in the beginning. About how ahead of her time she was, and how strong. He'd thought Barbara was like her. But after his mother had come to live at their house she'd realized that Daya Habeeba was ten times stronger than she'd ever be. Daya Habeeba didn't care what anyone thought – not her husband, not her children, not the people they'd married, and certainly not any Turkish airline officials. That's what Barbara had imagined anyway.

Now as she looked at the ruined wrinkled face, she had another thought. Daya Habeeba needed her. Before she'd never thought that. She had her children, she had her antics and her fiery old woman's spirit. But spirit resided in flesh. Habeeba's hand had the feel of a horned toad. Barbara remembered how shocked she'd been the first time she felt it. The first time Habeeba had brushed her lips and her cheek against Barbara's she had wondered how live human skin could feel like that.

Now as she drove along she felt Daya Habeeba's hand creeping over hers. It reminded her of the way she'd been following her around from room to room, trying to connect before she ran away.

"You fight man," she said, her gaze once more sharp as Barbara took her eyes briefly off the road.

Barbara nodded, feeling a little embarrassed. She really had made quite a fuss. She didn't know why she had done that. Certainly she wouldn't have if she'd had any idea Daya Habeeba was only pretending to be disabled.

In spite of herself, Barbara smiled. You really had to hand it to this woman. Given the life she'd led, most people would have given up.

Then with a shock, she felt Daya Habeeba's hand creep over her breast. She was so surprised she nearly swerved, but luckily she recovered and recalled a scene she had witnessed in the refugee camp. Several women had been hanging freshly washed laundry on any tiny tree or bush they could find. Instead of the usual intent expressions on their faces, these women had been having fun. Barbara could see that from the way they were laughing and poking one another in the ribs. Children were able to find fun in the camps, and even men had their moments, but it was a rare sight to see adult women laughing like that. Barbara had drawn closer. She wanted to understand what they were saying, but she couldn't. Then one woman had reached out casually and grabbed another woman's breast. She'd caught Barbara's stare and said in surprisingly clear English, "Look! She say we lesbian!"

At the time, she hadn't understood this woman's self-conscious remark. But now she got it. Women back there connected with each other in a far more visceral way than they did here. With effort Barbara managed to continue to drive, but inwardly she felt as if some barrier had broken.

She remembered Habeeba's eyes on her even in the camp. In England when she was growing up, her breasts had developed early. She hated the size of them then and always dressed to minimize their bulk. Not until she met Simail had she begun to feel at ease with being what used to be called busty.

"You like my own daughter," the old woman pronounced as Barbara pulled over into the right lane.

"Really?" Barbara said, thinking of the difficult Soreyya.

She glanced over to catch the smile on Habeeba's lips. "No," the old woman asserted, suddenly changing her mind. "You better!" Barbara put on her turn signal, preparing to exit the freeway. She knew this solidarity wouldn't last. Back at the house they would once again fight over turf. But for moment she could enjoy it.

As soon as she was off the freeway she reached over awkwardly and grabbed through the layers.

"Yaaaah," Daya Habeeba cried out.

For a split second Barbara thought she might have gone too far. But then, as she wended her way past the tract housing and cul de sacs, she heard the laughter start. A deep cackle that only later developed into a hacking cough.

Feast of Sacrifice

Ibrahim would never forget the day he found out he was going to America. The sun was shining hard as he came up the Corniche in his little Fiat, honking the whole way for joy. Not that anyone else heard him. Traffic on the Corniche was one massive din. But today Ibrahim didn't mind being another childish Egyptian. In exactly one month he would be leaving this mess and going to California.

He squeezed his car into a space on the side street and began walking toward his parents' bakery.

"Ya Ibrahim!" One by one the people in the neighborhood called out to him. Ibrahim was famous in this quarter, his quarter, which even had the same name, Ibrahimiyyeh.

If anyone had a radio or a television or a cassette player that was broken, they would bring it to Ibrahim. Before he finished high school he was known as the "Father of Electronics." Even after he got his degree in electrical engineering, he didn't turn away his friends. Ibrahim loved gadgets and gizmos. He always had, ever since he was a little boy, although no one knew precisely where this love had started or how he had learned so quickly the way to make these tiny, magical things work.

"Ibrahim! What are you doing here? Is something wrong?" His mother came out from the back of the bakery, the red flush from the heat of the ovens showing through the tan of her skin.

Ibrahim smiled, but she continued to worry. "What is it? Don't tell me. You're sick. No, you look too pleased with yourself to be sick. Aha! I know. Behira is going to have a baby."

"Mama!" Ibrahim hugged her, which was unusual for him.

"Now I know there is something wrong!"

"There is nothing wrong," he said, grabbing her beneath her thighs and hoisting her into the air. "There is nothing wrong at all."

"Put me down," she cried out, more like a young girl than a mother. "Ibrahim, you have gone mad. What will the customers think?

"They will think I am too happy," he said, putting his mother gently back down on the tiled floor. "I am going to America."

She wasn't laughing with him anymore. She wasn't even smiling. "Will you come back?" she asked, fixing him with one of her looks.

"Of course I will," he said, without allowing himself to really consider the question. "I am Egyptian."

"Sometimes I wonder," said his mother, shaking her head.

Behira wasn't ecstatic either, but she knew what it meant to him. She was his wife and besides that, a professor of English. As soon as Ibrahim had been invited by the American professor to apply for a job at his company, Behira had written to Stanford University. They had replied that they would be happy to call her a visiting scholar and let her attend as many classes as she liked, although without giving her any money.

After that wonderful spring day of acceptance to America, all the days blended together until the final day in late fall when the sea turned gray and the sky rainy. That was the day when he and Behira picked up their suitcases and walked toward the check-in counter at

Cairo airport.

It was raining in Northern California too, but Ibrahim didn't care. He kept glancing at the shops in the San Francisco airport. It was incredible how many things they sold. The sheer number of differentiated objects was unimaginable. Even the most useless souvenirs had a kind of magic to them. Ibrahim ran down the moving walkway and felt he was flying.

"Wait!" cried Behira, huffing and puffing to catch up. "Ibrahim! How can you have so much energy?"

It was true. he did have an extraordinary amount of energy—more than ever now that he had arrived in the land of his dreams. That morning he awoke without any feelings of jet lag and walked out of their motel and down El Camino to stare at the displays of calculators and computers. At the restaurants serving exotic food. At the furniture shops and record stores and frozen yogurt places. (Frozen yogurt! he marveled to himself.)

"Look at this," he said to Behira, who was just sitting up in bed and rubbing her eyes when he returned from his walk. He handed her a belt he had bought. At first glance it was just an ordinary belt: a piece of purple-dyed elastic with a little plastic heart on the buckle. But when you pressed the heart, it played a melody--the tune to a love song in English which Ibrahim couldn't quite recognize, but was sure he had heard before.

"Can you believe it?" he said to Behira. "This only cost two dollars. We can send it to Azza."

Behira laughed and shook her head. "Ibrahim, you are a child. We don't even know where we can eat breakfast and already you are out buying toys."

That was only the beginning of Behira's complaints, but Ibrahim didn't allow his enthusiasm about America to be dampened. Yes, the cost of housing was ridiculous--five times what they had imagined and they hadn't imagined it would be like Alexandria. Still, Ibrahim knew they would find a place they could afford.

Of course they would find a place! After all, this was America, not Egypt. No one, not even the poorest of the poor, had to live in cemeteries and on garbage heaps. Why, if it hadn't been for Behira, Ibrahim could have lived at work. It was certainly clean enough, and quiet enough. The bathrooms were beautiful, and there were even showers. There was no dust because the air was filtered, and people came to vacuum every single night. The electricity worked all the time. If he got hungry in the middle of the night, he could just go and insert money into the machine that would give him a can of coke and a packet of peanuts. It was just a little company by American standards, but it made sophisticated machines that could help American doctors do miraculous things.

Ibrahim was interested in the cures, of course, but he was even more interested in the way the machines were put together. A lot of people didn't understand this about him. Even after all those years of university, he was still basically the same boy who loved to fiddle with the insides of radios. He could sit for hours at his bench playing with tiny wires and chips and have no idea that time had passed. In Egypt after you got degrees you were supposed to tell other people what to do, to spend your days shouting into telephones and attending international conferences. But Ibrahim wasn't interested in that. There were so many new things under the sun and so little time to figure them out.

There was only one person at Aslan Systems who had any idea about where Ibrahim came from. When Ibrahim had been there about a week, Jeremy came by his bench to talk to him. "I can see you're one of those Third World wizards," he said right off.

Ibrahim looked up. "Those what?"

"I can see you're a genius!"

Ibrahim's face tingled. He had hoped for recognition, of course. Everyone does. But this was more than he had expected.

"I had good luck," he began. "Others who are better than me . . .."

Jeremy grimaced. "Come on. You don't have to be modest. It takes more than good luck to get here. I know how many engineers in Egypt would sell their mothers for a job at Aslan Systems and the chance for a green card. Besides, I can see that you work about twice as hard as anyone else around here, and this place isn't exactly filled with slackers."

Slacker. Ibrahim recorded the word and stored it away for future reference, all the time never taking his eyes off Jeremy's face. It was a handsome face in the European fashion. The bones jutting outward with little extra flesh to cover them. Cold blue eyes and reddish gold curly hair.

"Don't worry!" Jeremy touched Ibrahim's shoulder. "You know a lot of people here don't know how to relate to someone from outside California, let alone the Middle East. But I've been around the block, and I have the feeling you're going to be one of our most valuable people. Just keep on doing whatever you're doing. Don't let me get in the way."Then he got up and hurried through the space between the cubicle dividers.

Afterward, Ibrahim thought a lot about what Jeremy had said. The part about other people treating him differently because he was a foreigner didn't turn out to be true -- at least Ibrahim couldn't see it. People treated him fine. Unlike Jeremy, though, their acceptance of him was unspoken. They didn't focus on their differences but on what they had in common -- engineering, English, interest in sports. Jeremy liked to focus on differences. Still, Ibrahim liked him. He saw that in a strange way he and Jeremy were alike. In Egypt, Ibrahim had been an outsider. In Silicon Valley, Jeremy, with his interest in politics and his skepticism about technology, was the foreigner.

"You should go to Egypt," Ibrahim would kid him. "People there really care about the kinds of things you care about."

"Yeah," Jeremy said thoughtfully. "But not enough to do anything about them."

Ibrahim laughed. On that he and Jeremy could agree.

He and Jeremy started spending time together, eating lunch, going to each other's houses -- hanging out in the Egyptian style, talking and eating. But sometimes Ibrahim preferred the company of his less complicated colleagues. The blond and brown-haired boys with the fair skin and the clear, untroubled eyes. These were the real children of technology, not Jeremy. They were the ones who had learned to program when they were 10 years old, who thought nothing of staying at work until they tracked down every last bug in a program. Ibrahim was fascinated by the way most of them hated to be more than a few steps away from a video screen.

When they invited Ibrahim to go out for pizza and play video games, he always accepted, even though he could feel Jeremy's disapproval. Jeremy didn't understand what Ibrahim saw in people like this. He didn't understand either why Ibrahim bought a huge, outdated Buick station wagon.

"What happens if the price of gas shoots up again?" Jeremy asked, as they stood in the parking lot where Ibrahim was proudly showing off his new purchase. "These old tanks are awful. You can't steer them. If you want to buy something reasonable and cheap, buy a Fiat. Californians haven't discovered Fiats."

Ibrahim snorted. Buy a Fiat that no one in California wanted? In Egypt, all he could buy was Fiat. Here in America, he wanted something American. That was why he came here. He rapped his knuckles on Jeremy's new Volkswagen Rabbit, which was parked next to his station wagon. "You want me to buy one of these rubbishes, don't you?" Ibrahim joked.

Jeremy was in love with the Third World and the way people there thought small and conserved everything. What he didn't understand was that people conserved because they had no choice. The natural thing was to spend. All his life Ibrahim had been forced to be conscious of every little thing he used. Now he wanted to be unconscious for awhile. He wanted to be American.

He couldn't be quite as unconscious as he would have liked. Especially not where Behira was concerned. Behira didn't like the way he was so entranced by his work. She wasn't interested in meeting his new friends either. She complained constantly about the hours he kept at Aslan.

"In Egypt, at least the electricity failed sometimes," she pointed out. "Then you had to forget about your dear computer."

He knew being here wasn't easy for her. He tried to cheer her up by taking her on trips to Yosemite Park and the Grand Canyon. Sometimes he remembered to invite her to a movie or bring her flowers. But she continued to call him at work, nearly every day.

"Hello, Ibrahim?" she would say, as if she wasn't sure it was really him. "What time are you planning to come home tonight?"

Then, one day she called and didn't ask, first thing, when he was planning to return. "Guess what," she began mysteriously.

"I can't guess," Ibrahim replied, keeping his eyes on the tiny parts he was sorting on his bench.

"I'm going to have a baby."

"You are?"

"Yes, isn't that wonderful? Your mother will be so pleased. I'm going to send her a telegram."

"Wait!" said Ibrahim, wondering how it could all have happened so fast, without his knowing. "When are we going to have this baby?"

"Not for a long time," said Behira in a voice he knew was intended to soothe. "It's very early still. Only a month and a half."

Ibrahim looked at his calendar. "I didn't think we would have a baby yet," he began.

"Ibrahim, we've been married eight years. Everyone in your family thinks there is something wrong with us. I'm going to cable your mother. She'll be ecstatic."

"Let's wait on telling my mother."

"Why?" Behira wanted to know.

"I need time to believe it myself first."

When he told Jeremy, his friend shook his hand. "That's wonderful."

"But you and Marsha don't have child."

Jeremy made a face. "Marsha works 60 hours a week at her law practice. How could we have a child?"

When Ibrahim thought about it, he realized he agreed with the Americans. Why have a child if it interfered seriously with your life's work? It was not that he disliked children. Certainly he doted on his nieces and nephews. But there were already enough children in the world.

As the time for the baby grew closer Ibrahim found himself getting more and more nervous.

"If a baby dies right after it's born, the mother and father probably wouldn't be that sad," he found himself saying to Jeremy over lunch when Behira was in her seventh month. "Not the way you would be if the child were older," he added in response to the look of shock that had appeared on Jeremy's face. "I mean there just wouldn't be that much time to get attached to it, would there?"

Jeremy let out one of his embarrassed laughs. "You're asking the wrong person. But . . . ," he broke off and gave Ibrahim a searching look before he continued. "I don't think you should worry about it. Most babies who are born these days survive."

"Maybe," said Ibrahim, studying the refrigerator case holding chilled fruit juices and flavored spring water. "Even now you can't be sure a baby will survive."

Jeremy put his hand on Ibrahim's arm. "Ibrahim, this is America.

Your baby is being born in Stanford Hospital. You know the kind of equipment they have; we make some of it here; Chances are very, very good any baby born at Stanford will survive."

Ibrahim wasn't sure why he didn't feel convinced. The worry bothered him. It was like a little chink in the armor of his faith in America The fact that he'd had two brothers who had died when they were little shouldn't really enter into it. He knew Jeremy was right. And yet he still couldn't stop thinking about it.

The baby was born on the Feast of Sacrifice, the main holiday of the Islamic calendar. The day God released Ibrahim from his promise to sacrifice his son, Ismail. Ibrahim had always been fascinated by this holiday. What had the old Ibrahim seen that made him willing to give up his own son? What could have been worth such a sacrifice?

The holiday went unremarked at Stanford Hospital, where a demanding God like that would have been deemed cruel and unnatural. Behira was sitting up in bed holding the baby--a girl with a red-tan face and a thatch of black hair. Behira had named her Waheeda, which meant the unique, the one and only. Ibrahim said the word to himself. Waheeda.

That night when he left the hospital he drove to Aslan Systems and worked at his bench until dawn. He didn't even feel tired. Waheeda. Maybe she would be an engineer, too. Or whatever the best thing to be would be in the 21st century. Whatever happened, she would have American citizenship. She would always be able to come here to work, or study or just to live. She wouldn't have to be a Third World genius to do it.

When he returned to the hospital, he found out they had taken Waheeda away to do some blood tests on her. When they brought her back, the doctor asked to speak with them.

"Your daughter's bilirubin count is quite high," she began.

"Bilirubin?" Behira echoed.

"It's a measure of infant jaundice."

Behira and Ibrahim exchanged glances.

"Don't worry," said the doctor. "It's not all that unusual. Sometimes it takes a few extra days for the liver to start working properly. We want to put her under some lights that will help break down the hemoglobin in her blood until her liver starts working on its own."

Behira and Ibrahim nodded.

"It's very easy to treat," said the nurse who came to wheel Waheeda away in her Plexiglas bassinet. "If you were back in Egypt, you could just put her out in the sun. But here in the hospital, of course, we need to be more scientific." She gave Behira and Ibrahim a sympathetic smile, but only Behira responded. Bilirubin, thought Ibrahim, suspiciously. What a strange term. Why, if it was so common, hadn't he heard it before?

Waheeda's jaundice didn't go away as fast as the doctor had said it would. Every day Ibrahim and Behira asked when they could take their baby home, and every day the doctor kept putting them off.

"It seems to be going down," the doctor said cautiously. "But we really need to find out what is causing it. Otherwise you could have the baby at home, and the bilirubin might go up again. "

"They say something is wrong with her," Ibrahim expostulated over lunch with Jeremy. "But they don't know what it is. Maybe it's not even something real. Maybe they just imagined it with all their equipment. She doesn't look yellow, you know. She has never looked yellow."

Jeremy looked sympathetic. "It's science. They have to find a name for it whether they can treat it or not."

"So you think they won't be able to treat it?" Ibrahim stared hard into his friend's eyes.

Jeremy shook his head. "Ibrahim, you're talking to the wrong person. I'm like you. I never heard of bilirubin in my life."

Behira and Ibrahim decided to take the baby home. They promised to bring her back regularly for tests. The doctors still hadn't figured out what was causing the problem, if there was a problem. Ibrahim wasn't sure what to believe. Waheeda looked normal to him although he wasn't sure because he was afraid to look at her too much.

At least he could escape from the situation and go to work. Behira was with the baby all day. Ibrahim didn't know how she stood it. Three times a week Behira had to take Waheeda to the hospital for tests. When she came back, she would rock the baby for hours to calm her from the pain of having blood drawn from the soles of her feet.

But even Behira had her limits. One day she exploded. "All they want is blood! They don't think about how it feels to her. All they care about is their tests. Surely they must know what is wrong by now. But they don't tell us. Maybe they think they don't have to tell us because we're foreigners, Perhaps it is not for Waheeda's sake that they take all of this blood."

Ibrahim was frightened. Behira had never talked like this before. It wasn't in her nature.

He held his head in his hands at lunch that day. "I don't know what to do," he muttered, wishing that the refrigerator case in the lunch room wouldn't buzz so much. He was getting a migraine.

"I don't think you can do anything," said Jeremy. "It's one of those situations where you just have to wait."

"Wait for what?" asked Ibrahim in a sour voice. "For God? I thought in America you don't say *insha'allah*."

Jeremy shrugged and shook his head. "Even in America, we haven't solved all of the mysteries."

When the diagnosis came, it was hardly more descriptive or helpful than what had come before. Waheeda had a congenitally defective liver. She wasn't able to get rid of bile. They would have to do an operation to put a hole in her side so the bile could get out. Then she would have to go around with a bag attached to her side in order to collect it.

Ibrahim couldn't really picture it. How could a child grow up like that? How could they live in Egypt? They couldn't buy surgical bags there. They couldn't find doctors who would have any experience dealing with such a thing. Thinking about it made Ibrahim doubt once more that the whole thing could be real. In Egypt, they would have simply taken their baby home from the hospital, and that would have been the end of it. Waheeda sucked. She slept. She even moved her bowels. How could she be as sick as these American doctors were saying?

Ibrahim suggested to Jeremy that they eat lunch at a restaurant. He didn't want to talk about Waheeda's condition in the company lunch room. They went out to a taco place. Ordinarily Ibrahim loved

Mexican food, which reminded him of Egyptian beans. But today he wasn't hungry.

"They've started calling us from the hospital," he told his friend. "They're threatening to do the operation on Waheeda even without our permission."

Jeremy's eyes widened. "Who's been calling you?"

"The doctors," said Ibrahim. "And one lawyer, also, I think."

"What are you going to do?" Jeremy asked.

"I don't know," Ibrahim replied. He was afraid to say more. Maybe Jeremy agreed with the doctors. Maybe he thought they should do everything to save Waheeda, even at the cost of making her into a helpless freak. Ibrahim stared at his friend and wondered how far Jeremy's understanding could go.

That evening Behira told him she wanted to take Waheeda home.

"Home?" he echoed, wondering what Behira was talking about. Waheeda was home. She was asleep right now in their bedroom. Had Behira forgotten?

"To Egypt," said Behira "I want to take her home to Egypt."

"And the doctors?" he asked, not sure she knew what she was saying.

Behira averted her eyes. "There are doctors in Egypt."

When Ibrahim told Jeremy they were going back, Jeremy didn't say anything about Waheeda. All he wanted to know was whether Ibrahim would return to Aslan Systems.

"I don't know," said Ibrahim. The thought passed through his mind that after Waheeda died there would be nothing to stop his return. But he pushed the thought away.

"We'll hold your job open for the next six months," Jeremy told him.

"Thank you," Ibrahim replied.

When they landed in Cairo, they took a taxi to Alexandria. No one was expecting them. No one knew anything except that Waheeda had been born.

"*Masha'allah*!" Ibrahim's mother cried in a voice filled with happiness as they walked in the door. "You have brought the baby to me."

Behira gave Waheeda into her grandmother's arms. Ibrahim's mother looked up in a couple of minutes. "This baby--perhaps she is tired, yes? And perhaps everything feels strange to her. She has never been in Egypt before."

His mother was looking at the baby with a worried expression. Ibrahim's heart sank. It was true. Waheeda was sick. Even his mother could see it.

Behira told what had happened in America, from the time of Waheeda's birth.

"So you have decided American medical care is not good enough for your daughter?" his mother asked in a careful voice when Behira was finished speaking.

Behira began again. She told about how the doctors had stuck needles over and over into Waheeda's foot until she screamed, how long it had taken for the diagnosis and how unsure they were about it, how there was only a 20 percent chance Waheeda would even survive the surgery, let alone manage to grow up. They could not put her through that, and they could not put themselves through it. Better that Waheeda should die, if that was what God wanted.

"I see," said Ibrahim's mother, folding her arms in front of her. "And what makes you so certain this is what God wants?"

Ibrahim's mother served coffee to the relatives who gathered to see Ibrahim and Behira and their new baby. All Ibrahim wanted to do was to go away and lie down. But there was no possibility of that.

"What are you going to do about the baby?" One by one Ibrahim's mother, Behira's mother, Behira's sister, and her sister's husband, who was a doctor, asked the question to which Ibrahim and Behira had no answer.

"She is sick " said the brother-in-law as if he was giving out some complicated diagnosis Ibrahim couldn't possibly understand.

"Yes, I know she is sick," Ibrahim replied.

"And you are her parents," said Behira's sister in an accusing voice. Ibrahim just stared at her.

In the end, they really had no choice. They took Waheeda to Cairo and had the operation done at Demmerdesh Hospital. Ibrahim glanced at the piles of debris on the hospital grounds and at the goats wandering around the neighborhood. It was absurd to think that a place like this was going to succeed at saving Waheeda.

When the news of their daughter's death came, Behira couldn't manage to stop crying.

He couldn't bear it. "Please," he begged his wife. "Try to think of the future. We can have other babies. *Insha'allah.*"

Behira gave him a terrible look. "There is only one Waheeda. She is unique. There will never be another."

Ibrahim felt worn out. He couldn't escape into work because there was no work At the university they had assigned his courses to others. He wasn't supposed to come back for another eight months.

A couple of months after Waheeda's death, they all went for dinner at his mother's house. Behira's family was there, too. An enormous amount of food had been prepared. Even as he put the food into his mouth, Ibrahim knew he was eating too much. But what could he do? Here in Egypt, everyone ate—unhealthy starchy foods followed by syrupy, sugary desserts. No one exercised. He had tried running a few times along the Corniche, but the ridicule and the traffic had made him give it up.

The topic at the table was America. Or rather the inadequacy of the imports the American government was fobbing off on them. People made fun of the American-made buses that plied the Corniche and didn't even have proper mufflers. The inferiority of the American rice currently for sale in the government cooperatives was obvious to everyone who tried to cook it.

"Before, when the Russians were here, it was the Russians you complained about," Ibrahim pointed out during a lull in his brother-in-law's impassioned denunciation. "Maybe the problem is us."

"Of course the problem is us," said his brother-in-law. "But these super-powers are not helping us. That's all I'm saying. Nasser was right. We need protection from these foreign industries. Otherwise we will never get on our feet."

With those words Ibrahim got to his own feet and left the table. He fought the idea of lying down and going to sleep.

"I'm going out for a walk," he told the rest of them. "Anyone want to join me?"

But no one wanted to come, not even Behira. He walked for a long time. All the way out to Glymenopoulos and then back to Ibrahimiyyeh. While he walked, he turned his face toward the sea. He'd been walking along the Corniche and staring out at the horizon a lot lately.

When he came back into the overheated, overcrowded apartment, everyone looked at him expectantly. For a minute he felt confused. What were they waiting for? Then he realized. He had made his decision.

"I'm going back," he told them. "I'm going to finish out my time at Aslan Systems."

For long seconds there was complete silence. Behira stared at her lap. His mother looked at him carefully with her shrewd brown eyes.

"Congratulations," his brother-in-law finally said. "I knew you weren't happy here. Maybe when you get America out of your system, you can come back and be one of us."

Ibrahim refused to smile back. He would never be one of them. Didn't they understand that yet?

Only his mother knew. She was looking at him with a strange expression."America," she said, shaking her head. "Even after Waheeda?"

Ibrahim didn't say anything. He looked over at his wife.

"And Behira?" said his mother, following his glance.

"Behira will stay here. They have given her some classes to teach for the semester."

Everyone stared at him as though they were looking at a ghost. Perhaps they were. His spirit had already gone to America. If indeed it had ever left.

"Next time I come home, I'll bring a videocassette player. Then we can watch movies instead of having all these arguments."

His mother shot him a look.

"You don't have to go to America to buy one of those," his brother-in-law pointed out.

"I know," said Ibrahim. "But in America they have the best selection."

He closed his eyes for a second and imagined himself going up and down the aisles of an electronics supermarket. Sony, Panasonic, Quasar, Zenith, RCA, Toshiba, Mitsubishi, Hitachi. They were all laid out in front of him like a feast waiting to be consumed. He opened his eyes. His family was staring at him. They didn't see. They would never see. How marvelous it all was.

Áshura

The call came exactly one week after the incident in the village.
Even though he'd been expecting it, Matt still felt rejected.

"I don't understand," he said in a stiff voice. "If the government can
just toss people out, why do you send people here in the first place?"

His landlady, whose phone he was using, hovered around, eyeing
him curiously. Probably she had already heard that he was persona non
grata, or whatever that translated to in Farsi. It was 1975, and intercity
phone lines had just been installed. The connection was surprisingly
good.

Ken, the regional director in Tehran, a slow-moving Midwesterner,
waited for Matt to calm down. "If they want someone out, we don't
fight it."

"I don't know what you heard." Matt worked hard to keep the hurt
out of his voice.

There was a noise on the line that sounded like Ken sucking in his
breath. "Only that you insulted the Shah's mother-in-law."

Matt stayed silent, although he wanted to say "insult" was not the
right word. What he'd done was to give the dictator and his family a
taste of their own medicine.

"I know it's hard," Ken was saying now. "But don't make it worse
by taking it personally."

Matt felt the tears welling up and fought them off. How else could he take it?

"Listen," said Ken. "The expulsion order is for the 20th. That's the Shi'ite month Moharrém as you may or may not know. The tenth day, as luck would have it, is Áshura. You know what happens then, right?"

"Sure." Matt didn't want Ken lecturing him on the history and culture of this place.

"Well listen, if I don't talk to you again I want to wish you luck."

"For what?" Matt asked in a sour voice.

"Have a safe journey back," Ken said in a patient voice.

The line clicked and Matt stood there staring at his landlady, who was busy tightening her chador under her chin. She was an older woman, although hard to say how old in years. Life in this place aged people fast. She had several gold teeth in the front of her mouth, and wrinkled, leathery skin.

"'Good news?" she asked hopefully.

Matt shook his head. She followed him into the courtyard. "You will give me the rent at the beginning of the month?"

Matt said something reassuring and then ducked under the low door frame leading into his own courtyard. As soon as he got inside he stared at the books on his shelf. Most of his library had been left behind in the U.S. He had just a few treasured paperbacks by Franz Fanon, W.E.B. DuBois, and Herbert Marcuse. Books from the political science courses he'd taken in college. His father had expected him to go to law school right after graduation. He'd disappointed the old man by joining the Peace Corps. They said they were sending him to a village with a spanking new school, except when he got here he found it didn't exist. Iran is a very farce-ee country, the more jaded ex-pats liked to pun. Matt would frown at them at parties where he was only included because of being a fellow American.

That was back in October, when he would get up in the morning and wish he could ask for a transfer to somewhere else. Iran was too hard for him. Not for the reasons the other ex-pats hated it. They didn't like the way people here resented Americans. But to Matt that was perfectly understandable. How could you like a country whose government had completely re-ordered your history? A foreign government that had put a petulant playboy like the current shah in power? A tyrant who gobbled up all the resources while most of his people lived in abject poverty?

On his first visit to the village, Matt's heart sank when they showed him the room where he was supposed to teach. There was no window and barely even a door. It was nothing but a hovel, fashioned out of dried mud. But he put the best face on it that he could as he sat in the headman's house, sucking on sugar lumps to sweeten the bitterness of over-brewed tea.

The first time he saw "his boys," as he now thought of them, he'd thought they looked like candidates for special ed. Ranging in age from about eight to eighteen, their heads were shaved and most of them refused to even meet his eyes. Instruction got off to a slow start.

He hung in there for a week, as each day's attendance dwindled. Finally he stopped coming. He figured they would be relieved when he didn't show up. But he was still worried. Being a Peace Corps was technically a job, one that he would need a recommendation from when he went back to the Real World.

By the third day he was tired of hiding in his house, so shortly after noon he jumped on his motorcycle and headed out of town in the opposite direction from the village. The bike had been his one luxury, bought from a German tourist. He gunned the motor over dried-up stream beds, past springs with tell-tale patches of green surrounding them. Under the wide blue desert sky, he started to feel like himself again. The next morning he got out of bed right away when he heard voices outside. These sounds were followed by the creak of the gate opening into the courtyard. Through the window he saw a boy coming up the path, the chadored figure of the landlady beside him.

"The foreigner is in there," he heard her saying in her hoarse voice.

Matt wondered who exactly she was letting in. A passing salesman? The Iranian equivalent of the Jehovah's Witnesses? Or maybe it was SAVAK, the Shah's secret police, come to ask the foreigner what he was doing here. Although why they would do that was anybody's guess. Everyone in this country just assumed that all Peace Corps volunteers were CIA agents.

He pulled his pants on over his pajamas and went to the door. The shaved headed boy who stood there looked strangely out of context. The town was full of modern appliances, European cars, fashions from Paris. This boy with his baggy trousers and shaved head was either from the poor neighborhood near the bazaar or from one of the surrounding villages. He must be selling something, Matt decided, when he saw the red plastic bowl in his hands. People hawked things in the alley all the time – mainly kerosene oil, but sometimes fruit.

"Mr. Mattoo," he said in heavily accented English. "Why you not come to teach us?"

Only then did Matt realize that this was was one of his students from back in the village. It took still another moment to grasp what he was saying.

The boy's eyes – brown, large, luxuriously fringed in black – rested on him while his name – Ameer – popped back into his mind.

"I was feeling sick," Matt lied.

Ameer gave a solemn nod. "God willing you will feel better soon."

"God willing," Matt echoed. "*Beh farmayeed.*" He gestured for the boy to enter his room.

But no amount of inviting would bring Ameer past the threshold. Instead he handed the red bowl to Matt. It appeared to be full of sour-cream-like yogurt. In addition there was a little bouquet of fresh mint, tied with a blade of grass. Matt stood in the doorway watching for a long time after Ameer went away, carefully closing the crudely hewn gate behind him.

After that, Matt never missed another day. He went to that dark hovel of a classroom – so hot in the summer and now freezing in the winter-- and taught them anything he thought might be useful – English, simple arithmetic, how to read maps. He wrote to a friend in the United States and asked him to send a kit he'd had in his own childhood. Called a "Visible V-8" it was intended for American kids interested in working on car motors. Matt thought it might prove more useful than learning English. These boys in his school had no land of their own. Their families were serfs for the local landlord.

The fact that most of the engines here weren't V-8's didn't occur to him when he placed the order. When the notice of its arrival came, he told himself it didn't matter. At the very least they would learn the vocabulary items – pistons, cylinders, crankshaft. His heart swelled with enthusiasm as he headed over to the customs office where he hoped to convince the authorities that it was not anything of great value. Nor did it threaten the rule of the current regime. Those were the two issues that mattered the most.

Once they saw the plastic and realized it was what they called a toy, they saw no need to confiscate it. But the shiny packaging fired their imaginations, and they ended up charging him the whole price again in customs duty. He paid without complaining and took the now-opened box filled with plastic pieces back in a taxi. He hadn't wanted to compromise it by putting it on the back of his bike.

As soon as he got it to his room, he wanted to take it out to the village. Only then did he realize that it was already getting dark, and night was not the right time to arrive with a bunch of little pieces of plastic in a place with no electric power. Reluctantly he waited until the following morning.

It was winter now, but he woke most mornings with the sun in his eyes. It was warm on his back too when he went outside. Just as he was wheeling the bike outside the gate, Ameer hurried up the alley, on foot and out of breath.

"Mr. Qorbanipoor says you must come right away. Important visitors are coming."

Matt hesitated. Qorbanipoor's title was agricultural agent. But Matt had never seen him show the slightest interest in crops. He inhabited an office in town where he fielded calls that always ended in him shouting, "Qorbanet" into the receiver, literally, "I am your sacrifice," presumably to the people to whom he owed his position. Qorbanipoor was not his real name. But Matt enjoyed calling him that. "Son of sacrifice" seemed about right for a man who was ready to sacrifice nothing for the greater good, like so many of the people put in charge of things here.

Now Ameer was telling Matt how it was finally going to happen – what they had all been waiting for. The village would get the school that had been promised. They were going to break ground for the building today.

The February air entered his nostrils like a sharp herb as he kicked down the pedal of his motorcycle and headed out of town along the avenue of plane trees. Ameer hung on behind as they sped past the fallow fields of winter, Matt noticed once again how the sun made this ancient used up land, so full of erosion, and cracks, seem fascinating. He loved the weather here. One or two brief thunderstorms were the only breaks in a series of days that were framed in turquoise and azure.

Ameer hopped off before they came within sight of the village. Matt had been here long enough to understand what was going on. If Matt were seen transporting a mere student like Ameer, he might lose face. If Ameer showed up with his teacher, he might attract too much envy from his peers.

Matt got off his motorcycle alone. There were more people hanging about than usual. Children with dirt-streaked faces crowded around the motorcycle. It never got old. The arrival of the Peace Corps volunteer to their village was like the arrival of the afternoon bus. It gave them something to mark their days, something to look forward to. He smiled and waved the way he always did, and then he walked to the house of the village headman.

The men stood when he entered. The villagers had gaunt sunburnt faces and rusty black suits. The city men had paler skin and European worsted over thicker waists. After everyone sat down, the headman's daughter set a glass of tea on the rug in front of him.

"Thank you," he said, the words sounding unnaturally loud in the silence.

After the ritual greetings, no one said anything. But Matt could see from the way their eyes met – past him, over him, around him – that before he came, they'd had plenty to talk about. Matt kept stealing glances at his watch. Already these visitors were over two hours late. They were coming from Tabriz, to the north. It was part of a tour, a jaunt through the unwashed countryside. The royals, in the person of the Shah's mother-in-law, were engineering a series of photo-ops to show Americans and the rest of the world how much they were helping poor villagers. This was part of the Shah's so-called "White Revolution" where not only was the land supposed to be redistributed, the serfs were supposed to be re-educated. They might believe this in Washington, but Matt knew better.

Already he was starting to feel compromised, as if he were lending even more American imprimatur to what was going on here. Whether the school got built or not was not the point. The point was that this whole thing was a sham. He was not a real teacher, just a Peace Corps volunteer. As for the building itself, how many times had he seen government construction materials siphoned off from their supposed recipients? But of course he could say nothing about this. All he was supposed to do was sit and smile and look appropriately Western.

Ameer had disappeared. But Hassan was there, giving Matt an embarrassed grin and Bahman as well, over by the water spigot. Matt thought of the Visible V-8 back in town and wished he had brought it. He was on his fourth glass of tea when his thoughts began to race. Why was he just sitting here? Why didn't he just call his boys together and take them away to the spot where he usually taught them? Or better still, organize. Have a real demonstration. The village didn't just need the school that had been promised years ago. It needed medical care, clean water, electricity.

Once, after Ameer had reached out to him and brought him back to class, Matt had tried to teach them Pete Seeger's "Talking Union Blues" in pidgin Farsi. He wasn't sure how much they'd followed. Finally he had launched straight into the English.

"Now, if you want higher wages let me tell you what to do/You got to talk to the workers in the shop with you./ You got to build you a union, got to make it strong,/But if you all stick together, boys, it won't be long."

As he chanted he thought of the workers he had seen here. Men in the meagerest of clothes, barefoot some of them, throwing bricks to one another as they stood on rickety scaffolds.

"Talking Union Blues" had come from his earliest childhood. He had literally learned it on his father's knee. His students leaned forward, their eyes rapt as he intoned the lyrics. He felt some relief just saying the words. Otherwise it was too hard, feeling the injustices here and knowing the role his own government had played.

Later on Ameer took him aside. "We do not sing such songs in my country," he said with a pointed look. Matt felt a mixture of awe and shame. Awe that Ameer had understood. Shame that he hadn't realized he was putting them at risk. It was OK for Matt, the American, to hold such views but for his students to even be seen hearing them – that was dangerous.

Today Matt glanced around. A dung-fueled fire rose from the courtyard near where the women lived, the so-called "harem." Probably they had been planning for days, even months, the feast they were preparing. The chickens that had to be killed, the vegetables harvested, the bread baked in the underground ovens. Matt sat in the lone folding metal chair the headman owned and thought of how the villagers would go without for months in order to impress the people they regarded as their betters.

Finally, three hours after they were expected, a puff of dust rose down near the entrance to the village. No one had eaten for hours. It would have been impolite to eat before the visitors arrived.

The car came on slowly. A Mercedes, of course. The children, even the dogs, stood aside respectfully. As soon as it stopped, the driver jumped out and went around to pull the door open. A woman wearing a coat made out of some very rare animal stepped out into the sunlight.

"Welcome, welcome. We are your sacrifice." Mr. Qorbanipoor and his cronies moved forward as one body. Only Matt hung back.

Mr. Qorbanipoor had his arm outstretched. For a split second Matt imagined that he had taken the hand of the woman in the leopard skin coat, kissed it, and then pressed it to his forehead the way the villagers sometimes did with their overlords.

But then he realized they were just shaking hands.

"I want to present Mattoo Summerson," Mr. Qorbanipoor said. "He is doing very good work here."

The woman in the leopard skin coat actually took a few steps toward him. Matt looked down. Her shoes were high heeled with open work at the toes. He wanted to ask her if she had ever visited a village before today. If she had any idea of how the people here lived. Anger welled up in him. Anger at the way "his boys" had been treated. He felt the eyes of the villagers on him. Was he too going to be part of this charade?

Before he could think through the consequences, he had turned away. He didn't even see the expression on her plastic-surgeried face. He heard nothing. Just the pounding of blood in his ears at all the injustices that had piled up. He didn't see his motorcycle until he was almost on top of it. But once he was on and bouncing down the road, he knew he had done something unforgivable. This place was all about status, and power. No one even went through a doorway before determining the correct order of who should go first.

The call from Peace Corps central came six days later. Matt had not gone back to the village. Instead he had holed up in his room reading "The First Circle,"by Solzhenitsyn. He wanted to feel like a dissident but all he felt like was a failure. Now he would never be able to help anyone here. Never be able to plant subversive ideas. For a few moments he allowed himself to wallow in regret and self-recrimination. Then he pulled himself together and started throwing books into a suitcase. When he was nearly finished, a knock sounded on his door. He pulled it open. Ameer stood there, empty-handed this time.

"May I come in?" he asked.

Matt shrugged and went back to his packing. It was the height of rudeness, at least in this place. Not to offer words of welcome or tea, or even inquiries about a guest's health. But if Ameer felt insulted, he didn't show it. "Can I help you?" he asked, entering without even being invited.

"No thanks," Matt told him.

Still he didn't leave. "You will take the plane?"

"Train."

After Ken's call Matt had debated with himself. He might have flown if the Peace Corps Director hadn't been so insistent that he avoid Áshura. But the expulsion order had only ignited the old contrariness.

"I am coming with you." Ameer said in a way that was not a question.

Matt stared at him. After bringing the yogurt and the mint, Ameer had never acted as if he expected any special consideration from Matt. If anything he had seemed to steer clear of his American teacher and his dangerous ideas. The thought crossed Matt's mind that he might be working for SAVAK, assigned to make sure the disgraced foreigner actually left. Why else was he here? Matt didn't understand it.

"Ashura is day after tomorrow," Ameer reminded him.

"Yes, I know," Matt said.

"My father's brother lives in Tehran. You will be our guest."

It was a way of talking: this ordering someone to accept your hospitality. Otherwise they would be locked in a little ritual of refusal and insistence. Still Matt wondered. Why was Ameer so interested in him now? Matt studied him and then shrugged again. What did he care? The Visible V-8 was already in the hands of the trash man who had accepted the box joyfully and then stopped at the end of the alley to puzzle over the contents.

The next day the train station was jammed when Matt and Ameer alighted from their taxi, struggling with Matt's luggage. Matt had started having second thoughts when he found out there was only second class and they wouldn't have their own compartment. But it was too late. Flights out of town were all booked up. Ameer grabbed his heaviest bag and they climbed up to the car. Walking down the corridor Matt stared at the vintage wood paneling and oval-shaped windows facing into the compartments. Some of them were already being draped with the fabric of chadors for privacy.

When they reached their own compartment, there were no veils, and no women either. Even before he entered the little compartment with facing leather-covered upholstered seats, Matt could feel the eyes boring into him.

"Excuse us," he heard Ameer telling everyone as if Matt didn't speak Persian. "This is my teacher. He needs a place to put his books. He has many, many books."

The two of them pushed hard to get the suitcase full of books up into the luggage rack. Then the train started up.

"Where are you from?" a man wearing a tight fitting turtleneck under a shabby suit jacket asked him.

"Canada," Matt said before Ameer could translate.

"What are you doing here?"

"Studying poetry," Matt told them in Persian, ignoring Ameer's look.

Their jaws dropped, as if by not hearing the expected replies they had no idea how to go on with the usual barrage – how much do you make? Are you married? Why not?

Later, when he and Ameer had gone to the dining car sooner than accept the offer of cheese and bread from the man wearing the turtleneck, Ameer asked why he hadn't told the truth.

"It was the truth. I was born in Canada, and I love poetry," Matt told him.

If Ameer was surprised, he didn't say anything. Not until he had finished sucking the bones of the jujeh kebab Matt had ordered. Then he pronounced them not very fresh. Matt felt a little thrill at such rudeness. Even he knew that as Matt's guest Ameer was duty bound to praise this jujeh to the skies.

"Would you have preferred the dry cheese and bread that man was offering back in the compartment?"

"Don't worry," his student said. "The food at my father's brother's house will be like the food in paradise."

Walking back through the long swaying corridor behind Ameer, Matt felt off-balance in more ways than one. He still had no idea why Ameer had insisted on coming with him. Still less why he wanted to introduce him to his family.

Back in the compartment, mellowed out from the meal, Matt studied the others. The man in the turtleneck eyed him back curiously. He had a *zoorkhaneh* body. Matt had only heard of these "houses of strength." He'd never had the chance to visit one of these traditional all-male gymnasiums.

"American?" the man in the turtleneck was inquiring in English as if he didn't remember Matt's previous answer.

Matt sighed and then nodded.

"How long you here?"

Matt cocked his head, noncommittally, as if he didn't quite understand. He could see the man working hard to think of more words in English. But after a few seconds he gave up, and began talking to Ameer.

Matt listened, careful to make no sign he understood, as Ameer explained how Matt was his teacher and that he was accompanying him on a mission to Tehran.

"Why are you helping him?" the man asked.

Ameer shrugged. "The principal of the school has asked me."

Matt looked away, tired of trying to unravel why people said the things they did here. After awhile he closed his eyes. He was starting to think again about how his father would view this expulsion order.

In his younger days his father had been something of a firebrand too. Fighting for the rights of unions as a labor lawyer. But then, unaccountably, he had switched sides. Matt wasn't sure of all the reasons behind it. The obvious one, which his parents had already told him, was that Matt's grandfather had died and his father needed to take over the family firm.

"They specialized in corporate law," his mother had told him. "It was a wonderful practice. It made us a good living. You shouldn't judge him too hard."

But Matt did. He could barely remember that firebrand father, the one who now judged him too harshly. The one who had wanted him to go to law school instead of joining the Peace Corps.

Matt had never bothered to write his parents about the real situation here. So there was no way to explain about getting kicked out either.

Yesterday he had sent them a cable saying he would be arriving home shortly. He had no idea what reception awaited him.

The compartment had gone silent. Matt opened his eyes. They were all watching him. His heart pounded. What if he said the wrong thing? What if the men in his compartment decided he was really their enemy?

Matt had heard the stories Americans told about the things that happened to foreigners here. Three years earlier, an American in a neighboring town to his had had his throat slit on New Year's Eve. The ex-pats alleged the man was gay so it wasn't as frightening as it might have been. Being gay was still out of bounds in America as well as Iran. Still, what if someone just thought you were gay?

"They want to know if you like our music." Ameer was suddenly translating.

Matt looked at the faces turned toward him. "I love your music," he said simply.

Ameer started to translate, but the man in the turtleneck was already smiling and saying something back which Matt didn't understand.

Ameer said in English, "He wants to sing a song for you."

Matt felt surprised. Once in his class he had taught them "Old MacDonald," but they had all fallen into such fits of shyness and giggles at the idea of singing, he had had to give it up.

"Tell the man I would love to hear his song."

The man in the turtleneck spoke again. "Tell him it's a sad song, in honor of Hussein's martyrdom. For Moharrém"

Ameer nodded, but he didn't translate.

The song had begun. The first part was almost like an exercise, a warming up. Matt listened to it, thinking at first that it was nothing special. But then it grew on him as the clacking of the train wheels faded. The man had an incredible tenor voice, full of richness and vibrato. Matt closed his eyes, feeling his body soften as the music flowed through him. If only, if only, the music seemed to say. If only Hussein had not been slaughtered that day in Kerbala. If only the righteous had remained in charge of the caliphate.

The song spoke of the event that had fractured Islam on the nearby plain of Kerbala back in the seventh century. Matt knew only the bare bones of the story. How after the Arabs had conquered Persia, a group of men had brutally murdered Hussein whom the Persians had embraced as the heir apparent to the caliphate. Since then Islam had had two warring branches – the Sunni and the Shi'a. It had all happened in the lunar month of Moharrém, the name given to the "holiday" they were now "celebrating." *Ashura,* or the tenth day, was what Ken had warned him about. Matt had also heard the warnings of other foreigners.

"It's plenty weird stuff," more than one of them had said. "And the last thing they want is any of us witnessing it."

At the time Matt had still been distancing himself from those kinds of perceptions. But now he wondered if it applied to himself as well.

The song had ended. Once again Ameer translated. "He wants to know if you liked it."

Matt looked out at the pairs of eyes trained on him. For a second he started, feeling that they'd seen his vulnerability. But then he realized that what he was feeling, they felt also.

"Yes," he heard himself say. "I liked it."

There was another moment of silence. Then the spell was broken as they began pulling the seats out and sliding the backs down until it was like one big bed, covered in aging leather. They stretched out gingerly, draping their jackets over them. Matt lay between Ameer and the window.

Even before the dawn light cracked in beneath the shades he could hear people out in the corridor, lining up for the lavatory. Ameer was still sleeping. Curled up like a child under the cheap imitation American windbreaker he wore. Matt lay still as long as he could, willing himself back into the sleep induced by the rocking of the train and the singing of the song. He was too tired to get up. Too tired to do all he needed to leave this country. But it was too late. The day had begun.

He edged out into the corridor, feeling conspicuous. But no one seemed to notice him. They were too intent on getting their turn in the filthy toilet. When he came back to the compartment, without speaking he and Ameer gathered their things together. The train was pulling into the suburbs now, clacking past houses with bits of mirrors and colored glass stuck into their concrete facades.

In the big south Tehran station, the platform was thronged. But the mood had changed from the day before. In Tabriz, people had looked festive, their arms full of presents to take to relatives. Now they looked serious, almost angry. Near the platform huge black flags with colored calligraphy were stacked and next to them bouquets of chains, anchored in wooden handles.

"Follow me," said Ameer.

At first Matt followed blindly. Then he stopped.

"Where are we going?" he finally asked.

"My uncle has a stall in the bazaar."

Without explanation, Ameer quickened his pace. Others were running too. The stalls around them all looked closed, and Matt wondered why they were coming here. But he couldn't ask. Suppose someone heard his *khoreji* accent and caught sight of his obviously American-made clothes. The bazaar appeared closed. Shop after shop had the shutters pulled down. But Ameer pressed on.

Matt began to sweat. He would never be able to find his way out again. Not alone, anyway. These old bazaars were labyrinths. The rituals would be starting up soon. He didn't know the exact details of what would take place. But he knew it would be emotional, and he thought that it would probably start here. Finally they came to a shop where the shutter was not completely pulled down.

Ameer said something in Turkish into the dark and two men came out. Matt stared at them. They were swarthy-looking, with more stubble than Matt had. They wore hats, pulled down over their foreheads, and there was a Mafioso look about them that made Matt nervous. They grabbed his luggage and handed it in under the shutter to the inside of the shop.

"Ameer! Welcome! How are you? Are you well? *Salaam aleikum*," they cried, embracing him.

"My teacher, Mr. Matthew, has come with me."

Matt nodded politely, but the two men grabbed his hand in turn and shook it warmly. Ameer began talking to his uncles in Azeri Turkish. It was a language Matt barely knew, even if it was the language of the villagers. The Peace Corps had trained him mostly in Persian.

Matt sipped carefully from the tiny gold-rimmed tea glass they handed him, choosing a big lump of *qand* to hold between his teeth while the hot acrid liquid melted the sugar. He was waiting. Soon they would start offering him some goods. Rugs, probably. Or maybe jewelry. Hard to tell what they were selling here. But it wouldn't matter really. A foreigner, even an unemployed foreigner, ought to be good for some kind of sale.

Matt's vision still hadn't quite adjusted from the light outside. All he could see in the dimness were a bunch of burlap sacks. He recalled the time he had crossed the border into Pakistan and seen a couple of thuggish looking types carrying burlap sacks like these. A scent came to him. Something like turmeric. He'd never really smelled turmeric before Iran, but now its cool mustiness would forever remind him of the bazaar. The three men were talking among themselves. Abruptly they stopped and turned toward Matt.

They were looking at his clothes, his glasses. "I don't know," one of them was saying. "Are you sure?"   Ameer was gazing at him and smiling.

Matt's heart lurched. He put the glass down. "*Baw ayjahzay*," he said, using the polite formula for leave-taking as he stood up. He was already ducking under the partly closed shutter when he felt the ground shake. In the next second came the thunderous voices and footfalls of the marchers.

"Ya Hossein! Ya Hassan!"

Matt pulled himself hastily back into the shop.

Ameer came over to him. "Why are you trying to leave?" he asked in English. "You are my uncles' guest."

Before Matt could answer one of the uncles put his hands on Matt's shirt, a wool shirt, one of his good ones. A Pendleton plaid such as no Iranian would ever wear.

"You must remove it," one of the men was telling him.

Before Matt could say anything, the shirt was removed, and the four of them stared at the tee-shirt that was underneath. It was a faded McGovern campaign tee.

One of the men shook his head. Off went the shirt. Matt was shivering, from fear as much as cold.

But before he could make a move, the uncle had snatched off his glasses. "Don't worry," he said.

Then they pushed him out into the corridor where they stood on either side of him. Someone shoved a wooden handle into his hand. Attached to it was a bunch of small metal chains.

"Ya Hossein!" roared a new throng coming up behind them.

When they reached the rug shop, the four of them fell into step behind them. Matt was afraid to look from side to side so at first all he did was march. But then, gradually, he understood what the chains were for.

His throat opened and he felt his own voice joining the chant "Ya Hossein, Ya Hassan," that was punctuated by the rhythm of chains raised first to slap one shoulder and then the other.

Matt wasn't sure when he started to smell the blood. At first he saw it only on the others, blurrily, in streaks, running down men's faces, criss-crossing their chests. They were coming out of the bazaar then. The sun made the white garb of the men seem even brighter with the blotches of red blooming against the fabric. Matt felt something run into his eyes and put his finger up to catch it. Sweat, he had thought at first. But when he peered at his finger he saw it was stained in red.

By the time they came back to the shop, Matt wondered if the dizziness he felt could be from the loss of blood. But the wound turned out to be superficial although Ameer made a big fuss about it, dabbing it repeatedly with alcohol until it burned. Matt hooked his glasses back over his ears and stared at the men next to him. Their faces appeared disconcertingly close. He could smell their sweat too and their breaths.

"Are you OK?" Ameer asked, his face creased with worry. "Maybe we should take you to a doctor, yes?"

Matt shook his head.

Finally one of the uncles spoke.

Ameer translated. "My uncle wants to know if you are Musulman?"

The adrenaline was still pumping, but Matt could feel the fatigue underneath.

Ameer gave a nervous smile. "I tell them before, but they not believe. You understand our suffering."

Matt looked from one to the other of them, wondering what they really thought. Later, when he had his plaid shirt back on and they were out walking on the street to the uncle's house, passersby stared at his head bandage. Ameer held his hand, the way men did here. Matt felt utterly exhausted. But there was still a feast to get through. Everyone stood when he came through the doorway into the humble room where, judging from all the footwear neatly lined up on the mat, many bodies lived crowded together. All around him the conversation of the men buzzed, most of it in Azeri Turkish. But then the room fell silent and the oldest man there spoke. Ameer answered and then turned to Matt.

"He asks why you care so much about Hossein and the people of Iran?'

Matt looked around at the circle of rugged faces with jutting cheekbones and bodies with no extra flesh on them. He stared at the saffron-dyed rice still mounded on the serving platters and the sucked bones tossed on individual plates. He thought of the two story colonial house with pillars where he had grown up and the meals seated around the oversized polished mahogany table where no one spoke.

Finally he answered. "I don't know."

Afterwards when the answer was being repeated around the room he wanted to call it back. But Ameer was smiling and nodding at him as he told everyone sitting there what the American had said. The old man started to speak and the room grew silent.

"He says you are right," Ameer translated. "Only God knows these things."

Still later he felt relieved when only Ameer accompanied him to the airport. The ticket was there at the counter along with a note. "Let me know when you get back so we can arrange for another posting." It was signed, "Ken."

He felt momentarily reassured. So, the Peace Corps wasn't writing him off, only Iran, but then the black thoughts crowded in again. He didn't want to go somewhere else. He wanted to stay here. He thought of the times he had disobeyed his father. When he was little there had been physical punishment involved. But later on, the warfare had been merely psychological. Once when he had asked his father why he was aiding and abetting corporate greed, the old man had refused to talk to him for weeks.

He imagined his father's response to his expulsion. Have you helped anyone in this country by refusing to shake the hand of the tyrant's mother-in-law, if he really was a tyrant? As for the Áshura march, his father thought Catholic communion was barbaric.

Ameer wasn't saying much. Just sitting and waiting with him. Matt kept thinking of things he could offer. Maybe he should ask Ameer if he had any desire to study in America. Many people here did. But his student had never expressed such a wish, and indeed it was a long haul from a village school to an American university even if Matt could somehow help him.

The thought came to Matt that, in a way, the whole thing was like a relationship. In the beginning he had been repelled by Iran, the Peace Corps, the village. Then Ameer had shown up.

"Remember that day," he said to his student. "When you brought me that yogurt? Why did you do it?"

Ameer gazed at him with mild surprise. "My mother told me to do it."

"Your mother?" Matt exclaimed, thinking he had never met the woman.

Ameer smiled his secretive smile.

So many things Matt would never know, including what had impelled him to hit himself so hard, he broke his own skin.

Part of him agreed with his father and other westerners. These kinds of practices were barbaric. Iranians needed to pull themselves out of the Middle Ages. But there was another part too. A part that loved this land and this culture and these people beyond all reason.

Ameer was looking at him again, a questioning expression in his eyes.

"What is it?" Matt asked.

Ameer said, "I wish you could see the *taziyeh* tonight?"

"What is that?"

"It is a play to show what happened that day on Kerbala."

Matt laughed and then regretted it. Once again, he was distancing himself. So he said, "I'm sorry. I have no choice. I have to leave."

"I understand," Ameer said.

Again there was silence between them.

The flight was called and he saw Ameer aim an anxious look at the gate through which his teacher would go.

Once more he spoke. "Áshura," he said. "It is like our Union."

Matt stared at him. Surely he couldn't be serious.

But much later after he was already seated on the plane, he thought it over carefully. Yes. Áshura. It was the only day the current shah would allow people out onto the street en masse. The only day they would be able to gather without being shot at.

That was when he understood. As long as they were busy beating themselves, the government would steer clear of hurting them. As long as they were protesting injustices from centuries ago, they would be left alone. Goosebumps rose on his flesh as the plane lifted into the air. He looked down through the clear cloudless sky at the barren landscape ringed by mountains. For as long as he lived, an important part of him would remain in this place. He knew that now.

Crossing the Border

The first time they went to the clinic, the doctor wanted to know why they hadn't come in sooner. She should have been seen in the early months of her pregnancy.

"We have just come from a war," Sherko told him"We are refugees."

"Oh?" The doctor, who was still writing on his prescription pad, didn't look up. "From Vietnam?"

Sherko and Gizeng stayed silent. Everyone knew Saigon had fallen six months ago. Vietnam was one of the reasons it had been hard for them to get permission to come. Americans didn't want too many refugees from faraway wars. Unpublicized wars like theirs were the last on the list.

The doctor, who had a beard, looked up at them. Gizeng thought he resembled her brother, the one who was still back in an Iranian refugee camp. "You're not Vietnamese are you!" he said, laughing at his own mistake.

Sherko laughed too, to be polite.

"So where do you come from?" The doctor was looking back down again.

"From Kurdistan," Sherko said.

The doctor gave a brief puzzled look, but did not ask where that was."Here is your prescription," he said, standing up. "I know it's late to start you on vitamins, but better late than never."

He looked into Gizeng's face, and she felt more self-conscious than when he was examining her under the sheet. Staring into the tarnished mirror of the hotel bathroom, she had grieved for the lost beauty of her girlhood.

"I won't ask what your diet has been like. There's nothing we can do about it now. From today on, I want you to eat whenever you're hungry. Good food. Please, even if you don't have much money, spend what you have on food. Do you understand?"

"I always bring good food for her," Sherko said stiffly.

Later on, out of earshot, he complained about this doctor — how ignorant he was.

"Do women from Vietnam have red hair?" he asked in a disgusted voice."Do they have grey eyes? Maybe this doctor wants to send us back. Maybe he is just looking for an excuse."

The days passed. Sherko brought back food from the Yemenite restaurant where he worked. In Iraq he had been a lawyer, but here in Brooklyn he was only a lowly kitchen worker, taken on as a fellow Sunni Muslim.

Gizeng laid the food out on newspapers. Mostly bread and lentils, but meat too, which Sherko saved for her from his lunch. He worked long hours while Gizeng slept, or tried to sleep. There was no comfortable position. Not on the bare wooden floor of the hotel room and certainly not on the sagging bed. She longed for the floral print bedroll of her childhood, mattress and quilt both stuffed with the best wool. Or the *koorsi* where the whole family sat during the winter, the fire under the platform making them feel like bears in a den.

Gizeng looked out the window into the courtyard. There was no tree. No sign of natural life or green anywhere. Just blank walls and a few windows. Below were concrete and asphalt. Above, grey sky. When they first arrived, Sherko had taken her to a park. She had the idea of going out and trying to find that place again, but then felt afraid. She had never gone anywhere alone in this city.

Every week they went to the hospital. Each time a different doctor examined her. Sometimes a man; sometimes a woman. The "due date" they gave her came and went but there were no pains. No water gushing down her dress the way Gizeng remembered her aunt having. She felt heavy, and her back ached, but she had no sense of any baby ready to enter the world.

Today they were at the hospital again, her feet in the metal stirrups and the drape over her lower body. Gizeng steeled herself against the hands that palpated and probed. It was a woman this time, but that seemed to make no difference. These doctors here were efficient, but without warmth. The hospital was huge, with hundreds of people in the waiting room – many with more problems than a baby who wasn't coming. Of course the injuries from the Revolution, their revolution, were as terrible as these, but there was no hospital in the mountains where they could go to get treated. When the bombs fell, people died without medical intervention.

Gizeng hadn't imagined starting her family in this way. In fact she had urged Sherko not to come near her for months, which was easy enough. He was part of the leadership, away for weeks with the generals and the government-in-waiting. She was back in Iraq with his family. But then the bombing had started. She fled to Iran to be with her husband. That's when she must have become pregnant. They applied for visas. Everything she ate made her feel sick. At first she thought it was because she was away from her home, but then she realized she must have become pregnant.

"You may put your clothes on now, Mrs. Esfandi—yari." The nurse stumbled over her name.

The doctor came back in after she was dressed. The expression on her face made Gizeng's heart beat so fast she could not understand what she was saying.

Sherko translated."They want to keep you here and bring you drugs," he said.

Now she was really frightened. Why was this happening? In her family there had never been such a problem. The babies came from God. They "fell to earth." Human beings did not pull them out, and if they came out dead, then God had willed it.

"It is only to make the contractions start," Sherko explained."To help your body to bring the child out. You want that, don't you?"

They both felt awkward. Sherko should have been somewhere else, waiting with the other men for the women in his family to tell him about the birth of his son. She knew he hoped it would be a son, even though he never said this out loud. Gizeng herself didn't care. Not at this point. What difference did it make? A baby in a hotel room where they were eating on top of newspapers? She could not picture it.

"What do you want to do, Gizeng?" Sherko asked her.

"Wait," she whispered, and when he translated this to the doctor, she nodded and said, to Gizeng, "We'll try that first."

The pains finally started at night. The clenching and unclenching of

her body. When she stood up, liquid gushed out of her. She felt
ashamed to be on a wooden floor instead of dried mud. Sherko helped
her put on her clothes. Now she was clutching Sherko's arms as they
left the taxi and walked toward a building with hundreds, maybe
thousands, of lighted windows.

The doors opened ahead of them, as if by magic. They entered a
huge room, filled with people coming and going. The overhead lights
glared down. Gizeng moaned slightly as she sank into the chair.

"What is it? Are you all right?" Sherko leaned over her.

"Fine," she panted.

Sherko pointed. "I will go over there to sign the papers."

She watched him go, suppressing the urge to follow. At least the
pain distracted her from the fear about what would happen next, how
they would manage.

"We can go upstairs," he said, speaking in English as if he wanted
everyone to know their business. "If you are able to walk. If not, they
can bring a special chair."

Gizeng struggled to her feet. Of course she would walk.

The pain was so intense she closed her eyes in the elevator. Stories
she had heard of people caught by the secret police and tortured back
in Iraq filled her mind. Now she could only imagine the vengeance
they would take against the Kurds who went back after daring to rise
up against the Baathist government,.

When they arrived in New York City men in uniforms brought them
into a little room with no windows. Sherko argued with them in
English. Gizeng hadn't understood most of what they said. Later he
told her that he had shamed them, but Gizeng had not seen any

expression of shame on the blank-faced men who took their passports.

Now she followed him out of the elevator and down a hall where they came to a desk where a nurse in a white uniform asked for their names. As soon as they told her, the nurse got up and came around her desk. She put a hand under Gizeng's arm and said something in English.

"What is it?" Gizeng asked in Kurdish.

"She says she will find us a room," Sherko told her.

Gizeng looked into dark eyes that reminded her of home.

"It says here that you and your husband are refugees. May I ask from where?"

For the first time today Gizeng understood."Kurdistan," she whispered.

Walking down the hall, Gizeng felt the cramps intensify. When they got to the room the nurse showed her the bed and the gown and asked her to undress

"I will be back as soon as you have finished undressing. Then I will see how much your cervix has dilated. Do you understand what that means?"

Sherko looked away while she put on the cotton dress that was open along her spine. The sheets felt like ice against her skin. Sherko sat by the bed. She didn't want him to see her this way. They had argued about it earlier. But Sherko had said, the way he always said, "We have no choice, Gizeng."

When the Revolution collapsed, Sherko had listened to the leaders who said it would not be safe to accept the amnesty. He had gone before anyone else and sold her jewelry in the bazaar. She could still see the pieces he had laid out on the table — the filigreed 18-carat earrings and necklace of coins— all worth their weight in gold.

The nurse came in again and asked Gizeng if she wanted an enema. Neither of them knew what that was. She explained and then Sherko translated. Gizeng's face grew hot as Sherko's face turned red.

"It is as if they are trying to humiliate us," he said after she left yet again."Is she even a real nurse?" he added.

Gizeng stared at him. "You think she is not trained?"

"You see how she spends almost no time with us! Perhaps she is an agent the government sent to spy on us. You see the way she was looking at you? The way she wanted to find out where we are from? Also she is not dressed as the nurses are back in Iraq. Sisters, they call themselves. She is not a sister!"

Gizeng pressed her fingertips against the sheets. Sherko saw enemies everywhere. Back in Iraq it had been part of his job. But here she wondered how he could tell who was a friend and who an enemy.

As if she knew they were doubting her, the nurse came back. When she began to examine her, Gizeng held her breath.

The nurse noticed immediately. "You must not do that Mrs. Esfandiyari!" she said. "Breathe. Always breathe. It will make the labor pains much easier!"

As she straightened the bedclothes, the nurse said to them, "I was born not far from where you come from, a city in northwest Iran they call Urmia."

"Yes, we were there," Sherko finally said. "They allowed our people to flee to that city."

The nurse removed the earpieces for the stethoscope she was

wearing. "I have heard what happened. It is a shame." She leaned over Gizeng. "Is there anything I can do, Mrs. Esfandiyari, to make you more comfortable? My shift is ending and I won't be seeing you again."

Tears came to Gizeng's eyes. "Your people fought with us."

The nurse gave a faint smile. "Yes. Although we are Christians, we fought with the Kurds."

After she left, the room seemed colder. Sherko said, "Such a coincidence. An Ashoori nurse!"

Gizeng said to him, "Many different people come to America."

"Yes, I know that," Sherko snapped.

Gizeng saw him staring out the window. She wanted to get out of bed and stand with him. She knew how alone he felt. Ever since the Americans had come and announced they were withdrawing support from the Kurds, he had been like this.

"It will all be OK," they had told him. "You can work out a deal with the Iraqi government."

But no deal was worked out. Instead it was every man for himself.

The pains were coming faster now, but she was only halfway dilated. What if the baby was stuck? She wished she had asked the nurse what to do. In spite of her determination to stay silent, Gizeng whimpered.

Sherko came back to the bed, giving her a worried stare. The skin of his face appeared grey in the hospital light. His brown eyes looked a hundred years old. She couldn't remember what he used to look like, when he was still her *dastgirt*, the young, slightly solemn law student from the University of Baghdad.

"He is a good husband for you," her father had said. "This government will always need lawyers."

But they had rejected that government. And their own government didn't exist anymore. Not since the Shah had signed the Peace Treaty with the Baathists, and both Iran and Iraq had turned their guns on the Kurds.

Gizeng lifted her hand from the bed, remembering the feel of the turquoise ring set in gold filigree. She studied her pale bony wrists naked of the encircling security of the gold bracelets. The earrings had weighed so much she had to loop thread over her ears to keep the holes from ripping clear through. At the time of her wedding, no one was thinking of war. She had laid out the gold and stared at it thinking: what harm could come to a woman with such treasure?

The pains were coming closer now. The moan came out of her throat of its own accord.

"Please," she said to Sherko. "Can you get the doctor?"

"Maybe they will give you opium," he said. "It won't be good for the baby."

"Please, Sherko," she breathed.

She thought she heard him go out. To avoid thinking about being alone, she closed her eyes. Once again she was back in the mountains. Everything hurt. There were holes in the bottoms of her shoes, and her dresses were ripped. She wore three gowns. One was white tulle with gold embroidery. One was red sateen. One was made of purple filmy stuff with embroidered butterflies. Her best dresses. They had no value so she hadn't been forced to sell them like the jewelry.

She could hardly breathe. Her lungs were coated with dust, her insides dry and white like the bones of animals, or were they men, that they passed on the hillside. The war had twisted faces and bodies into forms that were worse than the most terrifying *deevs* of her childhood. She turned her eyes away from the bones on the mountains as she had turned from the aftermath of the bombs in the town.

She couldn't understand why she hadn't had a miscarriage. She'd eaten almost nothing for days. She couldn't remember a whole night's sleep. Sometimes she thought the pregnancy was a hallucination, or a tumor. When she got to a doctor, he would say she was mistaken. You imagine you will give birth, but there is nothing in you that is still alive.

The pain was pulling her back down the mountainside. Sharp pain that stabbed deep into her body. But the border patrol might be right behind them. Helicopters or MIGs could be up in the sky. They were like insects that had scuttled away from a lifted rock. When the rock dropped again, it would crush them into pieces.

"Push," Sherko was saying to her now in the dark. "You must push. The doctor says so."

She opened her eyes and shut them again. She was back on the plane they had boarded in Turkey. At the beginning of the flight, the hostesses had served sandwiches. The bread was stale and the cheese dry, but Sherko had crammed his in.

"Eat," he told her, but she left the food untouched almost until they had landed in Istanbul. When she finally put them into her mouth, the taste was awful, like the medicine the dentist had given her for her tooth in Iran.

"You must push," Sherko said into her ear. "Otherwise they will have to cut you."

Cut her? What was he talking about? Were they in prison? Was he warning her of torture?

She opened her eyes and then closed them again. When had she realized that Sherko was not the brave warrior, the Pesh Merga, the death-facer, he wanted her to think he was? He was as afraid as she was. Even more afraid. He had not been willing to die for what they believed in.

"Let's go back to Iraq," she had said when they were fleeing into Turkey. "We will go back and tell them what we feel. We will stand together for our country. If they will not give us our own land, we can at least die together. How can they kill us if we stand together?"

You don't understand, he said. We will not stand together. We will stand separately in prison. And you do not know what they will do to you. He had almost started to cry, thinking about what they would do to her.

The door to her room opened, and the doctor returned. Gizeng made an effort to come back to the present.

"He wants you to pretend that you are back in the village," Sherko was telling her. "Do what you would do there. Perhaps you should get on your feet. Maybe that will bring the baby out."

The doctor had guessed her secret. She was stuck in the past. But he couldn't bring back her village. That was burned to the ground now. The children who could not run fast enough were lying there still, on the ground next to the place where the mosque had been.

"Gizeng," Sherko cried now. "Please! For the sake of your mother. For the sake of your dead father. God rest his soul. The baby must come out or it will die."

"Die?" Gizeng sat up briefly before another contraction leveled her. Why had she never thought of the baby dying? Only of its not wanting to come out.

"We must go to another room," Sherko was telling her. Dimly she was aware of people around her talking, and of Sherko's attention diverted away from her. She felt the bed moving so she shut her eyes. When she opened them again they were in another room. This one had more equipment and a brighter light overhead.

'You must turn on your side," Sherko told her."So they can give you a needle."

She braced for the pain and felt relieved that it was mostly just pressure. Her legs floated out from her until she couldn't feel them any more. She remembered her wedding night. Her legs had been like this. Numb not with medicine, but fear while Sherko pushed into her.

"Push," Sherko said now, as if they had reversed roles.

But she couldn't push. She couldn't do anything. She closed her eyes. Once more she was back there. Ahead of them loomed another summit. She couldn't see what lay beyond it. She wanted to lie down on the rocks and give up. Their passports weren't real. They would be found out. Sent back. And if they weren't, what kind of life was waiting for them? She gazed toward the horizon of Turkey. Land that had killed hundreds upon thousands of her people. Something or someone was pulling her hard. She was on the edge of a precipice sheering off into a narrow valley, strewn with boulders. She would die for certain if she fell down there.

"Breathe, Gizeng, breathe!" Sherko called out.

The noise, when she heard it, felt along way off. She opened her eyes and remembered why she was here. She was having a baby, the one she had longed for even as a young girl watching other children being born around her. Hearing the cry of a newborn when there had been none before.She opened her eyes.The hospital lights glared down. She blinked, trying to accustom her sight to the brightness. The doctor had two long metal sticks which he began inserting.

She closed her eyes again and moaned. Why didn't they just cut into her? Wouldn't that be safer?

The doctor's voice seemed to come from far away. At first she thought she hadn't heard him right. But then they put the baby up on her chest. She had not heard a cry.

With great effort, she raised her head. "Is he dead?" In her language it didn't matter —boy or girl.

"No, of course not," Sherko said in English. "Alive! Praise God! Alive!"

Gizeng tried to look down and saw the matted dark wet hair. She felt the cord she had seen on other women. The one that had connected them. Then the doctor leaned over and cut it.

Sherko's face appeared above hers."Are you all right?"

"The baby" she said, struggling to sit up.

Sherko put his hand on her shoulder and pressed her back.

"Something is wrong!" she said in a loud voice.

"No, no," Sherko assured her. "The baby is fine. They must take her for testing." He spoke in English.

"I want to see the baby!" she said, still speaking in Kurdish.

"Please, Gizeng."Sherko leaned over her and translated what the doctor had just said. "They have to take the baby away for a little bit while you go to a special room to recover from the medicine."

"No," she said.

Sherko frowned. "No?"

"The baby must stay here."

Sherko and the doctor were looking at each other, but Gizeng didn't care. She took her free arm -- the one with no tube in it -- and held it down over the baby. They would have to cut her arm off to get this baby away from her.

"She will be all right," Sherko was saying. "I will go with her. I will never take my eyes off her."

Where had she heard those words before? Was it the promise Sherko had made to her before the Revolution started? Or was it the words of her dead father, saying he would never let anything bad happen to them?.

"Parwaneh," she whispered.

Sherko crouched close.

"I want to name her Parwaneh," she said.

"Upon my eyes," Sherko intoned in English. "It is your choice, Gizeng."

Parwaneh didn't cry as the doctor carried her away. That much reassured her, but it was not enough. They wheeled her into a place that was like a big refrigerator. Around her were lights and women, all kinds of women moaning. There were no babies.

At first she just lay there. She wasn't in the mountains any more. She was in this room. All she could think of was Parwaneh. How eager she was to see her and to know her. Little by little she felt the strength returning to her legs. Then she began to struggle. They had tucked the sheets too tight. But little by little she worked them off her. Finally she threw her legs over the side of the bed. A nurse had entered and came running over.

"Mrs. Esfandiyari! Stop!"

But it was too late. Her bare feet were on the floor. They stood back from her, as if they were afraid. She grabbed the side of the bed to steady herself.

"Where is my baby?"

This nurse was younger than the Ashoori nurse had been. She looked frightened. Gizeng thought of the village where they had grown up where everyone knew better than to take a newborn from its mother.

"Where?" she cried out in English.

"I will come with you," said the nurse.

If only she had been able to see Parwaneh ahead of her on the donkey trails they had followed through the mountains under cover of darkness. If only she had known that her daughter lay in wait for her as she huddled with the others in caves during the daylight. But she would huddle and hide no longer.

"I must see my daughter now," she told them as the nurse led the way down the polished floor of the hall.

"Gizeng! What are you doing?" Sherko was coming toward her.

"I am going to find her," she said.

"What are you talking about?"

But she pulled free of him. "I am going to find my baby!"

"Gizeng," he said in a warning voice.

But it was too late. Sun poured in through the windows. The floor was cold, but she didn't care. She could still feel the blood dripping out of her. Her legs felt stiff. But she would not stop now. She was finally ready to cross the border.

Familiar Stranger

Massoumeh ran her fingers over the design hammered into the brass tray. She could find the "Allah" part of it clearly, but the other part about Mohammed being his prophet was harder to trace. Perhaps with the rubbing necessitated by cleaning, the calligraphy had become less raised. Or maybe her knowledge of Arabic script was fading.

She moved away from the tray to the Na-een carpet. She could still feel the silken threads under her fingertips. She had brought it with her to California 15 years ago when she came here in the mid-seventies to join Hameed. The rug had been a present from her uncle. To sell in case of need. She had thought about that several times, but she was glad she'd been able to avoid it. Such carpets couldn't be replaced. The tray and the carpet were among the few treasures that had stayed with her all these years, and of course Donya.

Her daughter was on the phone. Massoumeh could hear her voice through the thin walls of the apartment as she stood in the little dining alcove. The sun felt hot already, even though it was only March. In a few more weeks Nowruz would begin.

When Donya was little, Massoumeh had sprouted the wheat herself in a pot they put up on the windowsill. She and Donya would peer through the glass of the aquarium at the five and ten cent store to pick out gold fish. In recent years they had dispensed with that. The goldfish were too hard for her to manage, and Donya didn't seem to care any more.

She heard her daughter's voice rising and falling through the thin wall that separated the living room from the single bedroom.

Massoumeh had no idea who she might be talking to. Donya's friends didn't come to this apartment. She met them at beaches and parks and restaurants where Massoumeh had never been, driving the car Massoumeh had bought her. Massoumeh thought of how when she was Donya's age the only place she had been allowed to go by herself was the few blocks between her father's house and her high school in the company of her girlfriends. Of course that had all been on foot, with a big square scarf carefully covering her hair and securely tied under her chin.

She felt her way over to the edge of the dining room table, pulled a chair out, and eased herself down. The heat was making the flesh under the synthetic material of her dress itch. She should get up and open the sliding glass door in case a breeze came. She felt a certain foreboding, as if the early heat presaged something. There had been rumors of funding cuts at work. Even though her boss had assured her that her job was safe, she still felt vulnerable. She couldn't work as fast as other people who didn't need special equipment to read. Luckily her screen reader worked with the accounting program. She knew of other blind people who hadn't been able to take jobs because their access software clashed with software they needed to do their jobs.

A closet door banged shut. Evidently Donya had finally gotten off the telephone. Massoumeh suppressed the urge to call out. In this apartment you could hear everything. That was why it was doubly important to give Donya her own space. Last month, Massoumeh had moved out of the bedroom so Donya could have it to herself. She and Charlotte had talked about this – how no one in Iran would understand the reason for such a thing. But as Charlotte kept reminding her, Donya had been raised here, not back in Iran.

The door was opening now. Massoumeh waited for her daughter to speak. Starting about a year ago Donya hadn't wanted to tell Massoumeh anything about where she was going or when she would be back. Several times she had slipped out without telling her anything at all. But the counselor had helped Massoumeh remind Donya about her need to know something, but not everything, about Donya's life.

"Baba called," she heard her daughter saying.

Hameed! Massoumeh's heart gave a thump. Why was he getting in touch all of a sudden?

"He's here." Massoumeh could hear the suppressed excitement in Donya's voice.

"Here? Where?" Massoumeh tried to tamp down her fears.

"At some kind of conference. The government sent him."

"The Iranian government?" Massoumeh heard her voice rising.

"Don't worry. He's not coming *here*."

She flinched at the note of disgust in her daughter's voice, then reminded herself of what Charlotte had said – that most teenaged girls were obsessed with image. Their cluttered little apartment in an unfashionable section of the city was never going to be seen as Massoumeh's heroic attempt to make a home for the two of them.

"So where is he staying?"

"Near the airport, at some hotel. I can meet him there."

Massoumeh nodded, but inwardly the fear grew. What if Hameed had a plan to take their daughter back to Iran, and what if this was what Donya thought she wanted?

"Will you see him?" Charlotte was asking her.

Massoumeh had told her news at the beginning of the session. Now she leaned forward, no easy task in one of Charlotte's chairs. Sometimes she thought Charlotte didn't want people to ever leave. The way she furnished her office with chairs and couches that were so soft and tilted back so far that it took all your muscle strength to get out of them.

"I don't know. I don't think so. She will go to see him at the hotel."

"How do you feel about that?"

Massoumeh didn't want to say that she suspected them of plotting against her so instead she remarked, "Strange. I think if we passed on the street we wouldn't even recognize each other."

As soon as she said that she knew it was wrong. She would recognize Hameed's voice anywhere – that nasal singsong with the metallic edge. She could hear it now in her imagination, chiding her. Massoumeh, why have you let Donya get so out of control?

"Is Donya eager to see her father?" Charlotte was asking.

"I think she is, but she doesn't want to talk to me about it."

During the pause, she felt Charlotte appraising her before she finally spoke. "Sometimes teenagers will reach out to the other parent if they feel the involved parent has judged them too harshly."

Judged who too harshly? Massoumeh wondered, but did not ask. She had been angry when Donya had been caught stealing. Is that what Charlotte was referring to? Donya didn't talk about Hameed much these days. But in previous years of course, Donya had asked a lot of questions. Massoumeh recalled telling her how after the Revolution, Hameed had gone from just being observant to being ultra-religious. How this had been contrary to everything Massoumeh believed. She remembered telling her daughter that Hameed had sided with the students who took the hostages at the American embassy.

"You mean he was one of the students who took the hostages?" her daughter had asked in an alarmed voice.

"No, no," Massoumeh had assured her. "Hameed would never have done anything like that." She understood how important it was for her daughter to stay on the right side of public opinion in America.

Now Charlotte was asking her why Hameed was coming at this time.

"That must be quite an honor, and an exception to the rules," Charlotte said when she got the answer about the conference.

"I think maybe Hameed wants Donya back," Massoumeh said carefully.

"Back?"

"I think he is angry at the way I kept her here."

Charlotte fell silent.

Massoumeh felt impatient. After Donya had been caught stealing, the court had ordered both her and Donya to go into counseling. Charlotte was a nice woman. But what did she really know about where Massoumeh had come from or what Hameed was really like?

"After he finds out what is going on here, for sure Hameed will want to take Donya away."

"Why do you say that?"

"In Iran, they always award custody to the father."

"But Donya is here."

"Yes." She bit her tongue. In the past, when she had tried to tell Charlotte what things had been like back in Iran, she had the feeling that the American woman regarded them as exaggerations. How could things be as dire as that for women?

"I don't understand," Charlotte persisted. now "Why would Hameed want to take on the hassle of a teenaged daughter raised in America?"

Massoumeh was silent. That was when the first bars of *Ghareebeh Ashena* began to start up in her mind. "Familiar Strangers" was how she would have translated it into English. How many years had it been since she had last listened to it? As a teenager she had played the cassette over and over as she daydreamed of how her life would change when she left her father's house. She thought of mentioning this to Charlotte, but it would have taken too much explaining.

When the session was finally over Massoumeh went back outside, feeling the sun on her face. She heard the bus pulling over next to the curb and stepped up to it, swinging her cane. Feeling her way past the driver she found an empty seat in front and sat down. She wanted to recapture the memory of the song, but there were too many distractions. The sounds of the bus doors opening and closing, the noise of traffic, and the loud music coming from someone's portable tape player. Donya kept pestering her to buy one, the kind kids her age kept plugged into their ears all the time. Massoumeh didn't think this was safe. Even if you weren't blinded, you needed all your senses to navigate when you were out in public.

She leaned toward the driver and asked him to tell her when they came to Lincoln Boulevard. It took forever to get around by bus in this city. But she couldn't afford to take taxis all the time, and she couldn't have Donya driving her everywhere either. Just last month Donya had talked about getting a passport. She said she wanted to go to Mexico. But now Massoumeh wondered if Hameed had already been in touch with her.

The bus stopped, and she heard the hiss of the driver pulling the doors open. Massoumeh descended cautiously, tapping her cane. She tapped her way toward a bench and then stopped to orient herself. Once again she felt gratitude for how carefully the American teachers at the blindness center had taught her to be independent. If it hadn't been for them, she would probably have been condemned to staying married to Hameed. As she walked, she took in the ebb and flow of the traffic noise as well as the conversations of people passing. At the intersection she turned right into the strip mall entrance two blocks from her apartment, making her way past the store fronts until the pungent aroma of spices wafted out.

"Good afternoon Mrs. Montazari," Mr. Rao, the proprietor, called out from behind the counter. How are you?"

"I am fine! Thanks be to God. And you?"

Mr. Rao chuckled. "Yes, we should always thank the gods, whoever they may be."

Massoumeh relaxed. Standing in this little grocery made her almost feel as if she were back in the Tehran of her childhood. The smells of the spices were slightly different than the ones she was used to and the Bollywood movies that played incessantly on the VCR were different from Iranian films, but the smallness and the friendliness were exactly like the baqqals back home.

"Here you are," he said, pushing the bag of basmati rice into her hands so she could feel it.

"Thank you," said Massoumeh, pulling the bills out of her wallet, carefully showing each one so he could check the denominations.

Walking home in the hot sun, she began worrying about Donya again. What if Hameed found out about the arrest? What then? Donya hadn't been formally charged, but she had been told to write an essay about how she would never do it again, and Massoumeh had been told she must go into counseling.

Back in her tiny kitchen, she carefully stowed the rice under the counter. Hands outstretched toward the boundaries of the walls, she made her way into the living room and began rummaging through the stereo cabinet. Finally she pulled the cassettes out en masse. She'd never had the patience to label them with Braille embossed tape so she always had to go through them one by one. Chastising herself for laziness, she clicked each one into the player, listening to a bar or two, before flipping it out. She went through five cassettes before she found what she was looking for. The beat started up immediately. The rhythm and the expansive introduction always made her think of traveling. She leaned back against the wall, tapping it out with her fingertips.

The sound of the orchestra died back and Googoosh's voice began, "You come from a strange city/ on a white horse with kindness you come...."

She closed her eyes and let the words wash over her, feeling herself when she was Donya's age, sitting in her room, wondering if a boy would ever come for her. Not just any boy either, but the Familiar Stranger.

"All this waiting brings spring with it! /How good to see you! /How good to wait for you! /How good to wash the dust from your body!"

How many times had she imagined herself waiting for him to come to her door – the Familiar Stranger on his white horse!

The spring she graduated from high school, Hameed's family had invited her family to a picnic in their garden outside of the city. The clouds of pink blossoms had been floating on the almond trees when she glimpsed the son of the old friend her father had promised her to when she was born. Hameed was older but not nearly so old as the men her girlfriends had been promised. Hameed was not fat. He was not balding. He had pale skin and fine features. His dark eyes seemed to take her in. He was smart too, whispering clever things in her ear while his aunt sat on the other side of them in the dark cinema during their first and only "date."

Even as she was staring into the wedding mirror, the candles flickering in the drafts from the hotel cooling system, Massoumeh was imagining Hameed as her own Familiar Stranger. The elevator took them to the room where the marriage was to be consummated. The light felt too bright and even with her clothes on she felt exposed. Hameed was not a stranger any more, but he was not familiar to her either. She lay back on the bed as she had been instructed and shut her eyes. When she finally opened them, she saw Hameed's reddened face straining above her.

"What is the problem, Massoumeh?" he was asking in an urgent whisper.

All she could think of were the family members waiting outside. She had to prove she was a virgin and somehow she was failing. Her heart began to beat too fast. Hameed went out and came back unsmiling, and handed her a packet of pills. It took a couple of hours for her muscles to relax. After that, there had been no problem, except for some minor pain and blood. In less than a year Donya had been born.

The voice on the cassette sang on, "How good to share our troubles as one! / I'll wait for your return/Even in prison, if we are together, I am free!"

The air in her little apartment was hot, but Massoumeh still shivered. Americans thought the Shah's era must have been better than the rule of the ayatollahs. In those days Iran had still been on good terms with the American government. But for ordinary people it was something else. How well she remembered how the secret police shadowed everything. Neighbors spied on neighbors. Prison came with torture, and worse.

Everything was life and death back in those days. She remembered how she would wait and wait for her husband to return safely to their little room, and how they would make love passionately. Just to feel alive in the face of repression and death was rebellion in itself. In America the zing had disappeared. There was no Shah and no secret police. Only the day to day tedium of diapers and Donya crying. Hameed had become fed up with his professors who, he said, didn't take him seriously because he was Iranian.

She stood up and went into the kitchen where she started pouring the rice out into a bowl. She would rinse it until the water ran clear. She didn't need to see it. She could feel with her fingers for when the starch stopped coating the grains. Out in the living room, the tape kept playing. Googoosh was singing one of the love-gone-wrong songs she was famous for. Massoumeh took the rice and threw it into the boiling water. The steam came up into her face before she moved back. As soon as the grains had softened she would pour them again into the colander and rinse them off. Then she would put the whole thing into a pot with butter.

She punched the little clock she kept handy to read out the time. Four-forty-five the mechanical voice said. She wondered if Donya was seeing him right now, and what they were saying to one another. Was she telling him how tired she was of Massoumeh and all her rules? Was he telling her that in Iran she would be treated like a princess? Hours later she finally heard the front door click open. The dishes were still piled in the sink. Massoumeh lay on the sofa bed wondering whether to pretend to be asleep.

Donya's footsteps paused and then headed toward her. "Maman," her daughter whispered. "Are you awake?"

She felt the springs give as her daughter sat down on the edge of the bed. "Baba sends his hellos to you."

Massoumeh felt the skin on the back of her neck prickle. Could it be that simple?

She said, "Please give my hellos to Baba. Will you see him again?"

Donya sighed. "He wants me to bring you to him."

The feeling at the back of her neck intensified. "When?"

"Tomorrow, He says he wants to talk to you."

"But what can we have to talk about?" Massoumeh felt as if she were the child and Donya the adult.

Donya's voice sounded vague. "I don't know. He didn't tell me. He just asked me to bring you there."

"What kind of conference is he attending?"

"You're not going to believe this."

Massoumeh reached out and touched her daughter's head. For once Donya didn't flinch, but let her feel the curls.

"Remember the conference we went to five years ago? The one where you bought the stuff you used to make the computer speak? That one."

Massoumeh took her hand away. Hameed had been trained as an engineer, but she hadn't imagined him designing devices for the disabled. Nuclear engineering had been his field.

"Hameed helps blind people now?"

"Not blind people," her daughter corrected. "He designs wheel chairs for the war veterans."

"War veterans?" Massoumeh echoed, trying to imagine her former husband caring about such a thing.

"From the war with Iraq. They have many people now in Iran who are disabled, and they are trying to help them lead useful lives."

Donya's tone sounded almost chiding, as if she knew the bad thoughts Massoumeh still harbored about her father.

Massoumeh said, "That's good."

Her daughter lay back next to her, putting her arm around her shoulder. "We talked about you."

"Me?"

"He wanted to know how you're doing."

Massoumeh felt her face grow hot. Hameed, interested in her? Probably there was something he wanted.

"What did you tell him?"

"That you're doing well. You have a job. You lead an independent life."

Massoumeh was conscious suddenly of the dark that surrounded her. Most of the time she took it for granted. But now she remembered the last time she'd been able to see Donya. Her daughter had been barely into adolescence when the diabetes had claimed her vision.

"Maman," she heard Donya saying now. "Why didn't we go back to Iran when Baba left?"

Ah! So that was it. Massoumeh had known the time would come when Donya would ask this. She had been so young when Hameed left that Massoumeh had been able to finesse it, saying only that she had wanted to finish her degree and then the war had interfered. Later on, when Donya was older, she had told her daughter that she and Hameed had argued about politics, and pretty much everything else. "We needed to separate.." Donya, an independent girl herself, had accepted this.

Now she heard the accusatory note in Donya's voice. "We could have gone back, at least just to visit. Baba said he was waiting for us."

"But I needed to work," Massoumeh said, hoping this wasn't heading in the direction she thought it was.

"You couldn't take a vacation?" Donya asked, sounding exasperated.

"In Iran, they consider the woman under the Iranian law, even if she has an American passport. I couldn't go, Donya. It was too dangerous. What if I couldn't get back here in time? I would lose my job."

"But if you were in Iran, you wouldn't have to work."

Massoumeh worked to keep her voice level. "Did Baba tell you this?"

"Yes."

Massoumeh waited in the dark. She had never told Donya what had really happened: how, when she was three years old Massoumeh had taken her to the airport two days before the three of them had been scheduled to fly to Tehran. They had flown to San Jose where they stayed in the apartment of a friend – someone Hameed didn't know. She was already losing her sight even then. She knew that whatever her fate would be married to a man she didn't love, the blindness would destroy her life.

Later on, she had heard from her family how he had called them in Tehran. "He was threatening to kill you," her sister said.

Once more Donya spoke, "Tomorrow is his last night here. Then he has to go to New York. He wants to see you, if you are willing."

The song came back to her. "How good to be with you! / How good to wash the dust from your body."

"OK," she said.

Standing in the hall in front of the mirror she knew was there, she thought of the mirror on her wedding night. It was important to look good so that Hameed wouldn't think he needed to mount some kind of rescue effort. She wished she had not gained so much weight, but it was so hard not to overeat, and even harder to exercise. She asked

Donya multiple times about the dress she chose until her daughter finally said, in an exasperated voice, "It's like you're going on a first date or something!"

The air in the hotel lobby felt cold against her face. She heard the voices of the conference attendees in the lobby and thought of the time she had come to this very same conference after graduating from the orientation class. How excited she had been to go around and sample the new technologies the vendors were offering. What a miracle synthetic speech was! The programs that captured not only text but pictures from computer screens and spoke them out to you had made her independent adult like possible.

"Selaam, Massoumeh," she heard Hameed saying, and then felt her hand grasped, not with one hand but two. Then he was kissing her on each cheek, before she could draw back.

The faint smell of his sweat took her back through the years and added to that something else — bad breath. So she was not the only one who had aged! His teeth had always been bad and he loved sugar too much.

"Baba said we can eat here at the coffee shop," Donya was saying, as if she needed to translate into English.

"We can go somewhere else," Hameed put in, using accented English. "But then we will have to get a taxi and it will be expensive. The government is only paying so much."

"This is fine," she said.

"Donya tells me you work for the government," Hameed said after they had squeezed into a booth. Donya slid in on her side. Massoumeh felt the warmth of her jeans' clad thigh.

"Yes, for the IRS," she said.

"You work for the agency that helps to spy on Iran?" Hameed said in an incredulous tone.

Massoumeh remembered how, in English class in Iran, a fellow student had once asked the teacher, an American, why it was *the* United States, but not *the* Iran in English. She had forgotten how Hameed was always on the lookout for such imagined slights.

"I stands for "internal" not for Iran," Donya explained in a disgusted tone.

"I didn't know you left nuclear engineering," Massoumeh said next.

Massoumeh felt Hameed stiffening up. The old fear came back to her. How he would lash out at her when she challenged him.

Donya said, "I think it's great you're doing this, Baba. Americans think all Iran cares about is building nuclear weapons."

Hameed gave a nasal laugh. "You should come to Iran, Donya. People there do not think such crazy things."

"Donya is an independent girl. It will be hard for her in Iran," Massoumeh said in Persian.

"Iran has changed," Hameed said.

"Oh yes. Now we must wear hejab," Massoumeh couldn't seem to stop herself.

"I want to come to Iran," she heard Donya saying. "But Maman needs me."

Massoumeh felt herself flushing as she imagined what Charlotte would say to this.

You need to let your daughter decide for herself. You should be careful of the demands you place on her.

"It is OK," she said now. "I am independent."

Hameed put his hand on hers. "There is no need for you to come alone," he said.

Massoumeh resisted the urge to move her hand away.

"When I first went back to Iran," he went on. "I was very angry at you."

She glanced toward the place where she thought Donya was sitting, but she heard nothing. Her heart sank. What if Donya was also mad at her? What if that's why they had invited her here – to tell her what a bad mother she was.

Hameed went on, "What you did was not right."

"But if I had not run away, you would have taken Donya."

"Maybe I would have," he said. "And maybe not. I cannot say. But a child belongs to both parents."

"Yes," Massoumeh whispered.

"And also to her country."

Massoumeh said, "Donya and I have both become American citizens."

"That's fine," said Hameed. "But does that mean she cannot travel to the country of her birth?"

Now she felt Donya's hand on her arm. Her daughter said, "Don't worry Maman. If I go there it will just be to see what it's like."

Massoumeh took a deep breath.

"Yes," Hameed reiterated. "She will see a place where women are valued not for their bodies, but for their souls."

"Their souls!" Massoumeh burst out. "What about *sighay*?"

"I don't see what temporary marriage has to do with any of this,"

Hameed said.

Massoumeh felt her cheeks grow hot. "All of it is about men getting what they want, no matter what they call it. No matter what price women have to pay."

"And did I get what I wanted when you took Donya two days before our flight and disappeared? Would you have been able to come to America if I had not gotten the scholarship?"

Massoumeh drew in her breath. She wanted to see Donya's face. How was her daughter taking this discussion? Did she remember all the arguments and worse?

"God has punished you Massoumeh, and for that reason I forgive you." Hameed spoke in the same old nasal voice he had tried to order her around with when they had lived together in California.

Donya was speaking. "That's not true. Maman has diabetes. She would have lost her sight in Iran too. Maybe she would have died."

"So," Hameed was saying. "You have raised her without religion."

Donya said, "It's not a matter of religion. I read the newspapers. I talk to my cousins. You don't treat women as equals."

"I?" Hameed said in a hurt tone of voice Massoumeh knew only too well. It was the same tone she'd heard when he started lashing out at her 15 years ago. The tone of rage after she got better grades than he did.

She heard his voice coming from above them as he stood up. "I see you have not learned anything. Not even now."

"Baba," Donya was saying. "Please."

"The worst is what you have done to our daughter," Massoumeh heard him say.

The waiter suddenly appeared. "Are you ready to order?"

"Yes," said Hameed.

Massoumeh held her breath.

"No," Donya said in a calm voice. "First I must read the menu to my mother."

The waiter disappeared.

Then Donya put her hand on Massoumeh's arm. "They have pasta dishes and chicken dishes and seafood dishes. What would you like me to read first?"

"The chicken dishes," Massoumeh said.

So Donya began to read in her strong, clear unaccented voice.

Hameed was still there. She could hear him sitting back down. But he didn't say a word as he waited for Donya to finish.

Taqseem

Sherry reached into her bag and pulled out her costume. The green glass beads she had sewn onto the bra glimmered under the fluorescent lights. She'd been so proud when she put it together last month that she'd almost shown it to Paul. Now she was glad she hadn't.

"Is that you Sherry?" Najwa's voice came from the sink area.

"I'm in here," Sherry told her, draping the low slung skirt over her hips.

"Tahir said to tell you he'll be playing a special taqseem tonight during the second set."

Sherry came out and asked Najwa to hook her up.

"He's very excited about it," Najwa said as she pressed her warm fingers into Sherry's back.

Tahir was always excited about his solo or *taqseem*, as it was called. From studying Arabic she knew the word was related to *qisma*, which meant "portion," a word that had come into English in the form of "kismet."

"He's talking about making a recording," Najwa was saying. "He asked me if we would let him sell it here."

"So what did you say?"

"Why not? If it makes him happy."

"Sure," said Sherry.

She had been excited when she first came here too, but mostly from the excitement of performing in front of an audience. She didn't have illusions about making it into any kind if big time. In fact, she preferred anonymity.

She leaned toward the mirror, applying foundation before outlining her eyes and lips. The redness didn't show as much after she glued on the false lashes.

Najwa glanced at her in the mirror. "Very nice."

"You mean for someone who doesn't have the right coloring."

Najwa shrugged. "In the Middle East the men love blondes even more than here."

Sherry's laugh had little mirth in it. Yes, that was what it boiled down to. Looks, not talent. But it didn't matter, she told herself. This wasn't her main gig. God forbid!

She walked down the narrow, linoleum-floored hall leading out to the main part of the club. That was when the doubts started to creep in. The words of a forty-something dancer she had met –a woman who had complained about her tips-- came back to her.

"It's just glorified stripping. All they care about is projecting their sexual fantasies on you," she'd declared bitterly. "As soon as they can spot wrinkles or cellulite, they couldn't care less how practiced you are."

She'd felt sorry for the woman. Now she felt sorry for herself. She hadn't received a single request for an interview despite the hundreds of CV's she'd sent out. What if Paul had tried to discredit her for working in a place like this?

She glanced around at the customers. The early show was either for people who wanted dinner or die-hard denizens. They sat at the little tables edging the dance floor. Some were studying menus. Others were talking to one another in the animated style peculiar to people from around the Mediterranean. She loved that style – so different from the repressed people she'd grown up with. She loved the food too. The appetizing smell of grilled meats slathered with garlic and onion and sprinkled with cumin and powdered sumac rose into her nostrils. Already her stomach was growling.

Luckily the musicians were getting out their instruments. Soon the uncouth sounds emanating from her belly were drowned out by the sound of a horn wailing and the chords of the accordion. A few tentative drum beats sounded and then grew into a steady rhythm. An oud string was being raised, bending the pitch provocatively. She moved into the no-man's area between the stage and the restaurant where cheap carpet could never be cleaned enough to keep her feet from turning grey with dirt.

Still, it was magic — the smells, the ambiance, the tawdry glitter. She was used to it now, but the first time she'd been almost paralyzed. What if someone from the university saw her here? What would they think? As if being a woman wasn't enough in this day and age when there were no female professors in the whole department.

The day of fear had passed. Her disguise had held. Or maybe there was no one who cared to bridge the gap between high culture and low. The Talisman became like a second home. She was more comfortable walking here than the barren corridors of Angell Hall. Najwa and her husband accepted her for who she was — a dancer.

Tahir gave a little nod and raised the clarinet to his lips. She came on slowly, the way she always did. Using her arms to make snakelike movements and lifting her hips, first one and then the other, taking tiny steps. Imperceptibly, the rhythm picked up. She moved the muscles over her rib cage, lifting her hands, and sliding her head sideways and then back and forth, still doing snake movements. She started rolling her shoulders in time to the music until her whole torso was undulating.

Some of the people watching stood up, stretching their hands toward her and moving their hips in synchrony with hers. She loved it when they did that. It filled her with energy so that when the band speeded up she didn't even feel it. She was shimmying faster and faster, the coins on her belt jingling. as the rhythms took full control of her body. Waves of energy welled up from her core, and then flowed out to her arms and hands.

When she was a kid she'd done ballet or as close to ballet as you could get in a town like hers. She'd loved it, but the teacher hadn't encouraged her, and her mother had gotten tired of driving her to lessons. She'd applied herself to school work, raking in the A's and regularly landing on the honor roll until she went to college on a scholarship and then graduate school on a fellowship. The belly dancing had been a lark at first, taken up almost on a dare. She'd had a boyfriend from Saudi Arabia sophomore year. He'd made it clear that their relationship did not have a future. But he knew how to dance. God did he know how to dance. Better than any female dancer she'd ever seen. He took her to clubs almost every weekend.

The dancing reminded her of what she'd forgotten – namely the stories she'd loved as a young girl. She would take the books out of the library, piling the tomes up next to her bed. The stories were set in the old cities of Baghdad, Cairo, and Damascus. In them jewels winked from every merchant's hand, meat was always succulent, and the unsuspecting traveler could stumble into a garden of delight at any moment. From her graduate studies she knew these translations from western travelers had been accused of cliché and worse —- ethnic stereotyping. But she also knew it was human nature to be captivated by the strange and the exotic. Here at the Talisman they catered to this. Besides, there were more Middle Easterners than any other group.

She wasn't thinking anymore about her stupid thesis advisor by the time she finished. She wasn't thinking about anything, except the people applauding her, standing up and throwing money or coming close and tucking the bills into her waistband. That was another thing. The people here were generous. They tipped tens and twenties, sometimes even fifties.

"Ya salaam! You were great tonight." Omar, the bartender, leaned over the black marble surface and spoke in a confidential whisper. He had smooth olive skin, perfect black hair and the features of his namesake -- movie star Omar Sharif.

"Shall I get you a drink?" he asked in a husky voice.

She looked into his liquid, lash-fringed eyes. "Thanks," she told him. "But nothing alcoholic."

"You are sure?" He flashed his cocktail shaker at her. "I'm making a dynamite cocktail tonight flavored with candied orange peel and cardamom!"

She couldn't help laughing at the way he always tried to get her high, as if the two of them were out on a date.

"What secrets are you two sharing?" Kamran, the green-eyed Kurd, leaned over to ask.

"We were talking about whether alcohol is necessary in order to dance."

"Of course not! To dervishes, dancing is itself a form of intoxication." He shook his shoulders as no American man would do.

"Then why are you drinking Johnny Walker Red?" she asked.

"Because I am not a dervish." He smiled and showed his teeth.

Omar took a juicer out from under the bar, put three oranges up on the counter, and cut them neatly in half. He pushed each one down onto the juicer and turned his hand, still pushing, while the juice spurted out.

Sherry watched, feeling hunger pangs already. She wouldn't really eat until after the second set when they would let her order whatever she wanted. It was one of the perks of the job. Once a week she got to savor the kebab or the kibbee, her favorite. She loved the way the crunchiness of the cracked wheat outer shell contrasted with the softness of the spiced ground meat inside. The Talisman wasn't known only for its belly dancing and drinks.

Omar glanced up and caught her eye while he poured the fresh-squeezed juice into a glass. His face wore a little smile, as if to say, I'm doing this just for you. After she drank it down, she twisted around on her stool and studied the clientele. The place was busier than usual. Maybe there were more people of Middle Eastern extraction in town, or maybe there was some holiday – the Prophet's birthday, the end of Ramadan, the return of the pilgrims from Mecca. There was always something. Or maybe it was just the rain. Outside it was pouring. The people coming in were shaking droplets off like dogs while Najwa practically grabbed the umbrellas out of their hands. Wet floors weren't good for dancing.

A couple that had just walked in caught her eye. The woman was wearing a long black coat that came down to her ankles. The man, who was tall, with blond hair, was helping her take it off. Then they turned around.

Sherry gasped. But before Omar could ask what was wrong, she was off her stool and heading out of the main room. She'd never seen anyone from the department here. This wasn't the kind of place that would attract a university crowd. For one thing, it was too far away. For another, it was a dive. The "s" was missing from the "Talisman" sign outside and the plastic flowers and cheap tables didn't inspire drop-ins. But there he was. She couldn't mistake him. And there she was, the famous former virgin.

Sherry hurried back to the shelter of the ladies room where she stood, leaning against the door of the stall, trying to figure out what to do. The more she thought, the more she kept hearing the words Paul had sprung on her last week. She'd known about Ameera's existence right from the beginning. Even before she and Paul had gotten involved three months ago, he'd told her there was this student back at the School of Oriental and African Studies who'd fallen for him rather badly.

"She'll get over it," he'd said airily. "Since I was her first."

For the last three months Sherry hadn't even thought of her. Then, last week he'd mentioned she was coming to see him in Ann Arbor.

"But I thought you weren't even involved with her anymore," she'd said like a fool.

He hadn't said anything, just taken her into his arms. Later when he was just picking up his briefcase from where he'd thrown it on her couch he'd turned to her and said hesitantly, "It might be better if Ameera didn't meet you."

Sherry looked into the mirror now and thought that if she started to cry again her make-up would be ruined. The door started to open and she fled into the stall.

"Sherry? Are you in there?" Najwa's voice reached her. "Omar said something happened."

Sherry came out. "I'm not feeling well, that's all."

Najwa's regarded her. "Does it have something to do with that man who just came in? The one with the Egyptian princess?"

"How do you know she's a princess?" Sherry went back into the stall, ripped off a piece of toilet paper, and blew her nose.

"It's written all over her. American University in Cairo. I'll bet you anything. Probably some relative of Mobarak's."

Sherry sniffled.

"Why don't you come out here? Hiding in there isn't going to make you feel any better."

Slowly Sherry undid the latch and came out. When she first started here Najwa, who was the wife of the owner, Hossein, acted cool toward her. Sherry didn't get it until one of the other dancers told her.

"In the Middle East, dancers are assumed to have loose morals. Most of the wives don't get involved in the business, but Najwa watches him like a falcon."

She watched Sherry too until she evidently decided she wasn't a whore, or at least she wasn't after her husband.

"That guy out there?" she said now. "He is a friend of yours?"

"Worse."

Najwa raised her bold black eyebrows.

Sherry had never mentioned she was a graduate student at the university north of Detroit. Najwa's gaze was fixed on her, so she said, "My professor."

Najwa's eyes got very big. "Oooh," she said. "And he wanted you to be with him in order to get a good grade?"

Sherry sighed. If only it had been that simple. "No, not exactly."

She thought of the conferences they'd had. How right from the beginning she had made the mistake of looking into his eyes. She didn't know why. Maybe it was because he was less threatening than the other professors. Maybe it was because he was actually interested in her work. She hadn't realized he was attracted to her until he started telling her these stories.

Like the one about a remote village near the Iraqi border where old men who were impotent would let their young wives sleep with unmarried peasants in order to have them conceive. She hadn't believed it. But he assured her he had it on the highest authority. Or about the men he'd met in another village in the mountains where the men said they had spent their last rials installing a water heater for the primitive public bath. When Paul asked why they were doing this, they said they had no choice. Their women demanded to be kissed "down there." She remembered too the way he had looked at her when he told her this and how she had gotten all hot thinking about it later.

Now she said to Najwa, "Last week he told me his girlfriend was coming, from England."

"She is his student too?"

"Was."

Najwa shook her head. "And I thought the people who study at the university were smart."

Sherry bit her lip.

Najwa said. "He knows you are dancing here?"

Sherry shook her head.

Najwa's voice was firm. "You must go on, not just for us, but for yourself. I bring you ice," she added. "For your eyes. And a special costume. I wear it myself, at home only. For my husband."

By the time she was dressed and made up Sherry could barely recognize herself. Her old costume was hardly shabby, but in this outfit she felt like the Queen of Sheba.

"Ya Salaam," breathed Najwa.

"I wish there were time to dye my hair."

Najwa shook her head. "No! You don't want to do that. She will wish for hair like yours."

When Sherry went out again, she stepped carefully. She and Najwa were about the same height so the skirt didn't drag on the floor, but she was wearing a contraption that wrapped around one ankle across the top of her foot and fastened on her big toe. Hanging from her ears were gold filigree earrings so heavy they dragged down her earlobes.

When she appeared, the drummer did a sort of fanfare which Tahir underscored with his clarinet. She rose up on the balls of her feet and peered toward the darkened table area. She couldn't see them, but she felt their presence. Only the feel of Najwa's costume gave her the courage to go on. But once she was standing there, her mind, which was usually full of her routine, suddenly went blank. She had no idea what to do next. She glanced over at Tahir. He nodded slightly and then began playing his taqseem. The other band members stopped so there was only the sinuous sound of the clarinet winding itself around the notes of the scale.

Sherry picked up her veil and used it to create a kind of tent around her face and shoulders. It was hokey, but it worked. She thought of Ameera sitting there in the dark, trying to divert Paul's attention from her, and she vamped it up, opening her eyes wide and staring out at them, her lips parting suggestively. When the music speeded up she literally jumped into her act and she didn't stop moving until Tahir put the clarinet down.

The applause lasted a long time, and then people started making that sound in the backs of their throats that people made at weddings and parties in the Middle East. At that point someone yelled "encore" and then everyone took up the chant. She felt lifted out of herself as she glided onto the floor again. She didn't even notice that the band wasn't playing. The beat was inside her now as she moved her little finger cymbals back and forth until they provided all the rhythm she needed.

Then Tahir stood up and started blowing on his horn. He would play a riff and she would respond to it. Play a riff and then wait. She'd never done anything like this before, but the crowd loved it. They kept it up until Tahir's face was red and she thought she might slip on the sweat that was dripping onto the floor. People whistled and ululated until she felt as if she were levitating.

Walking back to the dressing room, gravity pulled her back to earth. She thought of hiding and waiting until they closed or sidling around to the kitchen and leaving through the back door. But then she changed her mind.

She walked up to the bar where Omar said, "Whatever you want. You name it. Drink or whatever." She smiled and shook her head. Then she walked into the center of the room, and looked around. A couple of people handed her tips – tens and twenties. She finally spotted them in a corner. Ameera was facing away from her. But Paul was watching. She took her time coming over.

"Hello Paul."

"Hello," he said, his fair English skin blushing a deep red.

The woman sitting next to him had kohl rimmed eyes which she narrowed as she gazed at him, ignoring Sherry. "I thought this was the first time you came here."

The red in his face deepened and he even started to stammer. "I-I haven't ever come here before."

Ameera looked from one to the other of them. Paul craned his neck as if he were a giraffe, looking for a way out of the forest. Ameera's lips moved wordlessly.

"Ameera, this is Sherry Henderson. Sherry, my fiancée, Ameera El Any."

The word "fiancée" felt like a knife but Sherry kept her smile intact.

"Sherry is writing a dissertation on the power of Arab women as reflected in the folk tales told by villagers."

"That's not exactly it," Sherry corrected. "More like mirrored power. In the tales women can do anything. Travel to strange lands, fly around at night, take lovers, while in reality, as we know, their lives are quite circumscribed."

Ameera's eyes flicked over her. "So you are a feminist."

Sherry inclined her head.

"But you are also a belly dancer."

Score two, thought Sherry.

She went over to the next table and asked for a chair. She brought it back even though they hadn't asked her to join them. She leaned over so her cleavage would be visible, and said, "Paul tells me you're a student at the School of Oriental and African Studies."

Ameera's chin came up. "That's right."

"You're lucky," said Sherry. "Knowing Arabic already."

"I didn't know Arabic already," she said. "I grew up in England. I had to learn it."

Sherry said, "Well then you're in the same position as I am."

Ameera stiffened and moved her hand close to Paul's, but Paul was too shocked to notice her plea for solidarity.

He was gazing at Sherry as if he couldn't take his eyes off her. "Why didn't you tell me?" he whispered in a hoarse voice.

Sherry smiled. "I don't have to tell you everything do I? After all, I'm just your student, not your fiancée."

Ameera's eyes opened so wide, Sherry could see the whites all the way around her pupils. She wasn't bad looking. In fact she was quite pretty, but Sherry didn't want to focus on that.

"Excuse me," she said before she headed out of the dining room.

"A thousand thanks," she told Najwa handing her the earrings and the ankle bracelet. "You saved me."

"You saved yourself," Najwa said, dropping the jewelry into the pocket of her skirt.

Sherry went back to the ladies room. The elation was fading along with the endorphins. It would be a long drive back in the rain. She studied herself in the mirror as she wiped off the makeup. Her features were less than stunning and her body had its flaws. But what she'd learned from belly dancing was that if you kept moving people wouldn't notice.

When she came back into the dining room, Omar called out to her. "See you next week."

"Yeah, next week," Sherry called over the noise, Kamran turned and gave her a little wave.

The rain had let up but it was dark and cold and damp outside. The parking lot was full of puddles. She didn't like to linger. The neighborhood was not a good place to be a blond white-skinned woman after dark. For a second she flirted with the idea of running back into the Talisman, of letting the warmth envelope her again, of collecting the drink Omar had offered, and the meal she'd forgotten. She hesitated and then inserted the key into the ignition. The road was dark and wet. The drive took longer than she would have liked. But the music she put into the tape player — one Tahir had made just for her — kept her going.

In the Field

The village elders chose Mahmoud for me. I told them I needed someone to help me learn the local dialect. Someone who could sit with me daily, answering my questions, correcting my mistakes, breaking the language into little pieces so I could begin to understand. Before I left America, Richard, my thesis advisor, advised me not to have a special assistant in the field. Learn from everyone equally, he advised. But sit only with the women. The village will not understand if you spend time with men. I could sit with the women for five years and never capture one word of the gossip that flies back and forth between them like Morse code. When I asked one and then another to sit with me on a daily basis so I could learn, she would politely agree to do it, but never turn up at the appointed time.

Finally I figured it out: they were just too busy caring for babies, or cooking, or fetching water or herding animals. They had no time for a dilettante like me. So in the end I decided to ask the elders. I made a big point of saying I had a stipend from my university and could afford to pay for the person's time.

Doubts still remain. Am I breaking too many rules? I ask Sharifa, hoping she will clue me in.

"Ah Mahmoud!" she says, giving me a shrewd look. "He is a beautiful one. In America he could be a movie star, don't you think, Cindy?" Sharifa's grey eyes miss nothing. I wish I could see into the hearts of these Moroccan villagers as clearly as they see into mine.

I watch Mahmoud during our sessions. There is an area on his wrist where the sun has not turned his skin from olive white to rose tinted brown. I keep imagining the touch of his hands -- hot and dry and infinitely gentle, the way he is with his little brothers and sisters, and animals they herd.

Mahmoud and I sit together in my room every day for a few hours in the early afternoon. He conjugates verbs in Arabic for me. "He ejects, she ejects, I eject, you (masculine) eject, you (feminine) eject, we eject, you (plural) eject, they (masculine) eject, they (feminine) eject."

There is something weird about transitive verbs used intransitively, but Mahmoud has gotten used to my requests. He is wearing his djellaba. The coarse wool falls in folds from the chair that Sheikh Abdel-Azziz has managed to provide for me, the western woman. Mahmoud's face with its black eyes and dilated nostrils is always tense. But his body relaxes into the limpness of his garment.

When he comes to the end of "eject" he looks at me expectantly. "Other verbs? You want other verbs?"

It is a hot day. "The verb to plant," I say and then change my mind. "To break." I bite my tongue. I have to stop changing verbs. After all, Mahmoud can't read my mind.

"He breaks. She breaks. I break...."

I imagine Mahmoud on his wedding night. He probably won't marry until he's close to forty. His bride will be about eighteen. That makes her four years old today.

Outside there is a commotion. It is the hour after the noon meal when everyone is usually too groggy from food and heat to move.

A throng of children has gathered. Sheikh Abdel-Azziz and Mahmoud told them my work is important and should not be disturbed. Usually they obey. Now Mahmoud is talking with them in a heated fashion so so quickly I can't understand.

"What is it?" My heart rate has picked up.

Mahmoud's eyes which were drooping a minute ago are fully opened. "Your 'friend' has arrived."

In Arabic, with its second and third person genders, there is no mistaking the meaning of 'friend.' But who could have come to visit me here in the field, where my reputation has been secured with the appellation of cousin? Cousin to Richard, my advisor. Otherwise, how could I have known him? I am unmarried, by implication. Chaste, by necessity. I cannot know any men who are not related to me by blood or by marriage.

As I walk across the village, I try to collect my thoughts. Could it be Richard? If Richard had somehow come without letting me know in advance, there would be a great celebration. The slaughter of a sheep, excited yelling, and certainly the message that my mother's sister's son and not my "friend" had arrived. No, it can't be Richard. But who else could it be? My mind is blank. Who else could even find his way here?

When I get to the village square I am astonished to see Eric, my last fling before going into the field, leaning against the wall of someone's house. Eric looks exactly the way I remember him from Berkeley. His programmable calculator is still strapped to his belt. A clueless grin splits his face. He is wearing shorts made from ripping the extra fabric off full length pants, the threads unraveling over his bare hairy thighs.

"Hello Eric." I say coolly. I squint at him, wondering if I can make him disappear. Not just disappear, but erase all memory of him having come.

"Cindy." He bounds toward me in the dog-like way that used to please me in America where dogs were not considered unclean.

I step back just in time. "What are you doing here?"

"I thought you would be glad to see me," he says in an injured tone. "I hitched 200 miles in a broken down Mercedes truck to get here." He walks toward me again, as if he is going to embrace me in front of everyone.

"The people here think I am Richard's cousin." I step back.

"Richard's cousin?" He gives me a blank look. "Why?"

Hysterical laughter wells up inside me. But at bottom is fury. How could he have come here, with no preparation to the culture, no introduction, no invitation? After all the years I have spent getting prepared. Oh wow, I can hear him telling his friends back home. I'm going to see this chick I know who's living in a Moroccan village. She speaks the language.

"Imshi," I say in Arabic, knowing he will not realize how rude this is. Beat it. Buzz off. Get out of here. I can feel the entire village pricking up its ears.

"What?" Eric asks.

"You should have written before you came here. Or at least cabled."

"Why? Do they have a telephone office?" Eric looks around at the adobe houses. He can't see the eyes and the ears in the dark doorways.

"You shouldn't have come. Just your presence here could ruin everything."

"He is not my friend," I tell the others in Arabic.

In English, I say to Eric, "You should leave."

"But why?" he asks.

"It's time for my Arabic lesson."

"I can wait."

"Please don't."

"Shall we go inside?" I say to Mahmoud, switching back to Arabic.

"It's hot out here," Eric tells me in a wounded tone.

I ignore him and invite Mahmoud to come inside. I can see that he doesn't want to. The exciting new foreigner with his bare hairy legs and his red backpack is not moving. How long will Eric stay in the village? My village. Actually Richard's village. Perhaps he will stay and go hunting with Sheikh Abdel-Azziz. Sit in the men's guest house and drink mint tea. I can't stop him. Where men are concerned, it's a free country.

"The man who came here is a student at my university," I tell Mahmoud in precise Arabic. "I hardly know him. But he was traveling and thought he could come to see me. My department at the university should not have given him the name of this village." And I should never have gone to a field of black-eyed Susans with a wild-haired physics student I met in the A and P two months before I left for Morocco.

There is nothing else to say. At least nothing I can say to Mahmoud who is looking at me in a way I can't interpret. We return to verb paradigms.

The next day I am sitting with the women when I realize it is time for our session together.

"I'm sorry," I say. He is already sitting in my room, which he has never entered before without my express permission.

"The verb, 'to dig,'" I prompt him. As usual, verbs are not what I really want to know. What I really want to know is what the village is saying about Eric and me. I don't even know when Eric left yesterday.

Mahmoud doesn't say anything. He lays his hand over my hand which is resting on my notebooks. His hand feels drier than I imagined it. But it is not an unpleasant dryness. It is the warm dryness of a fallen leaf in the sun or the cracked desert earth.

I withdraw my hand. "Did you tell the others what I told you yesterday?" I ask. "About the man, Eric." I wonder if I should say the word, "Eric." Maybe to refer to him by name is to acknowledge our intimacy.

Mahmoud nods.

"He is not my friend," I say, knowing I cannot afford to repeat myself. If once was not good enough, no number of times will suffice.

"Yes."

Yes can mean anything here. Mahmoud is looking at me. All of me. Head, first. Then neck. He lingers for a long time on my neck. Then my chest. Finally he is at the place where I cross my jeans-clad legs.

I stand up.

Mahmoud stands too. He is taller than I am. For a second I stare at his lowered eyelashes. I have never seen such lashes as the people have here -- long, curled, thick, incredibly black. Mahmoud is standing so close that if I move we will be touching.

"I don't feel well." I back out of my room, into the hot sun. into the place where the whole village can see us. No one appears to be looking, but I am not fooled. I have seen the flash of white retreating at eye level from the edge of shadow.

Mahmoud follows me outside.

"I think I'll go to the city and find a doctor, " I tell him.

He doesn't seem surprised. "Shall I come with you, to the city?" he asks in a low voice.

I consider the idea as I walk down the rutted donkey tracks. Mahmoud is standing and watching me along with a throng of children. But I only look back once. After that, I walk deliberately toward town.

Now I am staying in a dilapidated hotel, trying to get the courage to return. Town has its own problems. There are other foreigners here, but none of them are women living alone. Only after I got here did I realize that Eric might be here too. Probably Mahmoud and the villagers think I have a rendezvous with him.

The men who hang around the hotel watch me. I watch the people who pass on the street. Once I thought I recognized Mahmoud by his walk and the way his hair grows on the back of his skull. But when he turned and saw me looking at him, I realized he wasn't Mahmoud. It isn't good to be caught looking at men you don't want to be accosted by.

At night I can hardly sleep, wondering if someone will knock on my door, wondering if the manager would use the other key.

I have an erotic dream. Mahmoud is standing outside my door. I pull him inside, afraid that someone will see him here. Then I imitate an Egyptian singer crooning for her lover. "Ya habibi, ya habibi."I gesture for him to lie down on the bed and slowly I begin to lift his djellaba. The dream ends and I awake in a sweaty mess of fear and longing.

Every day I wake hoping I will know what to do. But today -- five days after I ran away from the village -- is no clearer than before. I can't bear the idea of going back to America. Once I admit I couldn't hack it in the field, my career in anthropology will be over.

I alternate between sitting in my room and going down to the lobby. Sometimes I sit in the local coffeehouse drinking mint tea and eating pastry. Wherever I go, the eyes of the men follow me. Only men have the right to sit in public and watch people.

Back in my room I begin yet another letter to my advisor.

Dear Richard,

I know you aren't going to believe this.... That goes in the wastebasket.

Dear Richard,

*I used to think going into the field....*Crumpled.

Dear Richard,

Things are going well with my field work. I've made a lot of progress on the dialect they speak here, and the women are starting to tell me what is really on their minds. I don't know how anthropologists manage without knowing the language.

Last week I decided to make a trip to town and stay over for a few nights. It's a change from village life. Hot showers. Restaurant meals. The chance to read week-old copies of Le Monde. I remembered what you said. When you feel the lines between you and the people you are studying start to blur, you might try going away for a few days. That was valuable advice.

Now I feel ready to return and make real progress on some of my research questions. I'm sure I'll see all kinds of things I never noticed before.

By the way, you mentioned in your last letter that you might drop by if you get a travel grant. Perhaps I can save you the trouble. If you want any tapes or information, I'll be glad to send them. Not that it wouldn't be a treat to see you. But it might be better not to show up. The boundaries between men and woman, as you let me know, are pretty serious here.

That's all for now. I have to walk back to the village today and the sun is already getting high.

Ma'a salaama,
Cindy

I address an envelope and pick up the letter without putting it in. On the way to the post office, I hold the letter in front of me, re-reading it at least half a dozen times. That was valuable advice, I say to myself more than once. Then I return to the hotel to check out. On the way out through the lobby, in front of a dusty aquarium filled with murky, algae-suffused water, I run into Eric. Half a dozen pairs of hotel lounge eyes focus on us while we stare at one another.

"Hello Eric," I say finally. The reproach in his eyes is too much even for me, the field-hardened anthropologist.

"So you're admitting you know me," he says in a strained voice.

There really is nowhere to talk. Not in the lobby in front of this fish tank. Certainly not upstairs.

"Do you want to have a glass of tea?" I ask him. "I was just on my way back to the village."

"Are you sure you don't have something more important to do?" he asks as we sit in the cafe together.

Do the men in this cafe know the men in my village? Even a ten year old boy idly passing by could relay the message that I am here dallying with the mysterious stranger.

"The people in the village think I'm celibate." I spell it out for Eric. "I'm not supposed to know any men."

"Know in the Biblical sense?" He leers at me. He has devoured the *milles feuilles* pastry. Now he is licking his forefinger so he can pick each tiny

remaining flake off his plate.

I glance down at my lap. There are several flakes, but I'm not eating them.

"So how are you supposed to know that advisor of yours? What's his name?"

"Richard."

"Yeah, Richard. You slept with him, didn't you? Before you slept with me."

Trust Eric not to have driven me to the airport, but to remember every last thing I ever told him about my sexual history.

"Yes," I say evenly. "But that was before I became a grad student in the department."

"Right," he says. "That's how you got that fellowship, isn't it?"

"The people in the village think we're cousins," I say evenly.

"Ah. And I suppose cousins never make it here, huh?" He moves his forefinger in and out of his fist just to make sure I know what he's talking about.

I know I should go, but I'm desperate for real conversation, after all these weeks of telegraphic Arabic.

"Do you think the people in that village really imagine you're a virgin?" He gives me an incredulous smile. "Do you really think they know that little about you or about America?"

"It doesn't matter what they imagine. What matters is how I present myself. "

"And how is that?'

"As a person who doesn't sneer at what's important to them."

Eric snorts. "God! You've got it worse here than you did before. It's that guy Richard, isn't it? He's filled you full of this bullshit, and you believe it. Anthropology's an art, not a science. Be yourself, Cindy! They'll accept you."

Be myself or what you want me to be, I ask myself silently. There's no point in saying it aloud. I stand up.

"Hey, where are you going? I thought we were having a conversation. Maybe we could spend some time together. You know, go to Fez and a few other places while I'm here."

"I'm not on vacation."

"No?" Eric looks up, shading his eyes against the sun. "Sure, I get it now."

"Get what?"

"I could see you had something going with that guy who was in your room back in the village."

He said that because his pride is hurt, I say to myself as I thread my way out of the teahouse over the feet of the men who are all still looking at me. But even if I know with my head that Eric is crazy, I feel like I am the one going mad.

"In North Africa" -- I can hear Richard's voice as if I am back in Angell Hall listening to one of his lectures --"there are only three categories of women. One is unmarried virgin. Two is married woman. Three is prostitute. Oh yes -- there is a fourth -- madwoman."

It is the specter of the madwoman that haunts me now. I can see her, as Richard described her, setting out for the heart of the desert, turning her back on the people who manage to survive and multiply in this harsh landscape. No one has mentioned any madwomen to me since I came here. Maybe they refrain out of politeness. Or because they think I might be one. The essence of the madwoman is that she has deserted her own culture to live only for herself.

The dried mud contours of the village rise up in front of me. Dogs and little boys come bounding out. I smile my careful anthropologist's smile as I search their faces for signs of welcome. They smile back. There are no stones in their hands.

I walk down the main path of the village. The women are still hanging out wash, going for water, nursing their babies, and giving me, the western woman with no such chores, secret glances and sideways smiles. What are those smiles made up of? Superiority? Envy? I wonder if I will ever know.

Back in my little room, everything looks just as I left it. I can't believe they didn't come here and handle my things, wondering how many days would have to pass before they could claim my sleeping bag, my drinking cup, my tube of toothpaste for their own impoverished households. But the intactness of my things reassures me. I must still be under Sheikh Abdel Azziz's protection.

A shadow falls across the sunlight and I look up in alarm to see Tahir, the sheikh's right-hand man, standing in my doorway.

"Welcome," he says in his deep voice.

I nod and manage to smile. "I went to the city. I saw the doctor. He said I needed a rest," I explain quickly in classical Arabic.

He nods gravely. "We knew where you went. Mahmoud told us. He said perhaps you were ill. Are you ill?"

"I was a little. But now I am well. Praise God."

"Praise God," he echoes.

He continues to stand in the doorway, neither coming into the room nor stepping back out into the sun. He does not lean against the door frame, but stands erect, like a soldier ready to march into battle.

"The sheikh wanted me to ask if you need anything here, if you are happy."

The unexpectedness of the concern brings tears to my eyes.

"Because if you are not happy," Tahir adds quickly. "You must tell us what you need."

"I am fine," I whisper. "Absolutely fine. I am very grateful for the help of Sheikh Abdel-Azziz and of everyone in the village."

Tahir nods, taking in my tears and my attempt to hold them back. He seems about to depart when he thinks of something else. "We understand that you are far from your home and from your family. And that such a thing must be very hard for a woman."

Then he is gone, without the usual goodbye. I throw myself down on my sleeping bag. I have cried many times since coming into the field, and before, during those last confused months with Eric.

This time the crying doesn't last as long as the other times. When I get up I feel refreshed. I walk out of my room, ready to converse with Sharifa, if she is available. The sun is getting lower, and the breeze carries a faint hint of evening cool. How clean the air is here. Cleaner than any place I have ever lived. The sun at noon bleaches everything to blinding white. By late afternoon color and perspective return. I take a deep breath and stare at the pastel mountains in the distance. Once they seemed unexpected and alien. Now I like the way they limit the horizon.

Black Seeds

Azziz loved going to the Armenian store. They didn't go there very often. It was more than half way to Ypsilanti and cost a lot more than the supermarket. But when Azziz got there he would inhale deeply. The store made its own *lahmajoons* and you could smell them -- the minced lamb mixed deliciously with garlic and tomato -- as soon as you got in the door.

This night, though, Azziz was in a hurry. He was too shy to ask the owner to help him, so he searched frantically up and down the aisles, past the packages of flat bread and jars of pickled garlic. Black seeds. He'd consulted both Dr. Jeem and Annabel on the name in English. Finally he saw them. The spices were in large jars behind the counter, and Mr. Mamoulian, who was the only one who could weigh them out for him, was deep in conversation with a customer.

Azziz felt nervous. Annabel was waiting. She hadn't wanted to come here. It was a favor, Azziz knew. A favor to let him get the black seeds he needed to put on the bread he made for them. He was looking at the cardamom seeds when he noticed them moving around, almost like larvae. He glanced toward Mr. Mamoulian who was still talking with the customer. The last thing Azziz remembered was a sick feeling in his stomach.

When he woke up, he was spread full length on the floor. Azziz lifted his head. There was a dull pounding in the back of his skull. He squinted at the light. People had gathered around him. He gazed at their faces. Someone was coming over— a woman with red hair and a little boy holding her hand. She was so tall that for a moment she seemed like an alien goddess from an ancient religion. His vision cleared. It was Annabel and Jacob. Now he remembered. He was in America, not Turkey. Somehow, with the smells, he had thought ....

Annabel was talking in her high, clear voice. "We were out in the car. He was just coming in to buy black seeds."

Mr. Mamoulian nodded. "We must call a doctor."

"A doctor?" Annabel looked at her watch. "It's after five."

"You can take him to emergency," someone else said.

"Yes, of course," Annabel replied quickly.

They talked some more but Azziz couldn't follow what they were saying. His head ached, and the cold tiles were beginning to chill his body. He made an effort to get up.

"Easy does it!" a man with a heavy beard and a kind voice boomed.

Azziz blinked. Mr. Mamoulian reminded him so much of the principal of the school he'd attended. But no, it wasn't possible. That man hadn't been Armenian.

Annabel's forehead creased with its familiar worry line. "Azziz, are you all right?"

Azziz pushed the palms of his hands against the tile floor. "I think so."

"We were just trying to get some black seeds," Annabel repeated to the people who were still gathered. "Azziz likes to put them on the bread he makes for us."

"Black seeds?" said Mr. Mamoulian, moving back behind the counter. "I'll get some."

By the time Azziz was standing, Mr. Mamoulian had measured out a generous portion in a little plastic bag.

"How much do I owe you?" Annabel asked.

"Nothing." Mr. Mamoulian bowed slightly. "Nothing. Please."

Azziz felt woozy, and his stomach hurt. He forgot to take one last delicious whiff before they went out the door.

In the car, Annabel turned to him. "How are you feeling now, Azziz?"

His head ached, but he thought that was probably because he had hit it. "OK."

"I can drop you off at the hospital. I won't be able to go in with you, because I have Jacob. But when Jim gets home, one of us can come and get you."

Azziz felt a stab of panic. He hated going anywhere alone here. But the hospital seemed particularly frightening.

"I'm OK. By God, I'm fine," he said in Turkish.

Annabel adjusted the rearview mirror. "Are you sure?"

"Yes." Azziz spoke in English this time.

Later that evening Dr. Jeem came climbed the stairs to the little attic room and knocked.

"Please, you are welcome," Azziz called out, scrambling to get the covers off.

"No, no, please. Don't get up for me." Dr. Jeem stooped to walk under the door frame leading into the room under the eaves. Dr. Jeem was very tall. Almost two meters. But it wasn't just his height that stood out. It was his large nose, and the prominence of his forehead.

"What's all this I hear about passing out in the Armenian store?" Dr. Jeem chuckled. "I know the smell of *lahmajoon* is powerful, but surely not that powerful."

Azziz laughed. Dr. Jeem's sense of humor was famous. Everyone knew about it. Dr. Jeem loved Nasreddin *hoja* stories. People in the village would save their stories all winter just to tell Dr. Jeem when he arrived in the summer with his notebooks and tape recorders.

Dr. Jeem bright blue eyes bored into him. When Dr. Jeem was interviewing people, he would get this look. As if he were trying to see into the person. Into their very soul.

"Have you been eating OK?"

Azziz nodded. "Better than OK. Since I am in America, I am getting fat."

Dr. Jeem laughed. "And who is to blame for that? Azziz, on your cooking we're all getting fat."

Azziz waited. His employer's lips had parted when far away, downstairs, came the call. "Jim. Jim? Are you up there?"

"We'll talk again," Dr. Jeem said hurriedly. "Meanwhile, tell us if there's anything we can do for you. Annabel will take you to the doctor's tomorrow."

After Dr. Jeem left, the room seemed colder. Azziz knew it was silly to wish that his boss would stay. Dr. Jeem was a busy man with all kinds of demands on his time. It was amazing that he paid attention to Azziz at all. No Turkish employer would have bothered. It was Annabel's job to see to their servant. Still, Azziz craved more. He even had this feeling that if Dr. Jeem had come to Mamoulian's with him, he would have kept him from fainting. But that was ridiculous. Dr. Jeem wasn't a real doctor. Only a doctor of books and letters. Azziz lay back. At least the bed was comfortable. The most comfortable bed he'd ever had. There were at least five pillows and a big puffy quilt. He'd been amazed the first time he saw it.

"Is this for me?" he'd asked.

Annabel had smiled then. The old smile. The one where her blue eyes crinkled at the corners. Annabel had smiled like that all the time when he first knew her. Azziz hadn't met Dr. Jeem's wife in the village. Dr. Jeem came to the village alone to do his research. Several years ago he began going to an island in the Aegean for a vacation when his research was done. His family would fly out from America to meet him. That's when Azziz came to work for them.

Mornings he would watch Jacob. Afternoons he made dinner. He could still remember the kitchen of the villa. The white tiles and the place where the tiles fit together and the blood from the meat he prepared dribbled down into the grout. How he had loved cooking that summer! For their last dinner together he had made swordfish kebap and mussels stuffed with spiced rice.

After Dr. Jeem took the first bite, a smile had engulfed his face. "Azziz you've surpassed yourself."

Azziz could still feel the blush that had spread over his own face. He didn't know why Dr. Jeem's high praise made him feel so strange. It was like alcohol, or very strong medicine. It felt good -- very good at times -- but it also scared him. Their invitation scared him too.

"Would you consider coming to America with us?" It was after the dessert he'd made. Fresh figs over ice cream.

Azziz had sat there, the pleasure coming up in waves. Maybe he'd drunk too much wine. Maybe he was imagining things. But no. Annabel was seconding the invitation. He'd never thought of going to America. The idea had just never occurred to him. But now here were these wonderful people saying that they would pay his way over and a small salary while he lived with them and watched Jacob.

"And of course," joked Dr. Jeem in Turkish. "We wouldn't mind if you cooked for us."

"Yes," said Annabel. "And you could also learn English."

He didn't think about learning English as the rural bus bumped over the dirt road taking him back to his village in eastern Turkey. The other passengers looked at him with respect. They saw he was no longer just Azziz, but Azziz-who-was-wanted-in-America. He looked out through the big window, but instead of the parched plain he saw the green trees of Michigan. Dr. Jeem had showed him pictures of them and of a wooden house. The bus stopped and Azziz swung down, holding tightly to his two suitcases. The one in his right hand was the one Dr. Jeem had given him.

The children spotted it immediately. "You have goodies for us Azziz?" they clamored. They patted the new suitcase with their grimy little hands. "Did the Americans give you a lot of money?"

Azziz laughed. "Don't touch them," he warned, putting the suitcases down. But his gruffness was playful, and soon he was digging into his pockets. He had brought candies for all of them. He stepped into the dark doorway of his father's house while the children stayed outside. He watched as they squabbled with one another in the sunlight.

Then, slowly, his eyes adjusted to the dark. After the island and the villa, the sight shocked him. How small it was! How dirty! He stared at the threadbare rug which just barely covered the beaten mud floor and at the pile of mattresses stacked in the corner.

His stepmother came through the doorway, her eyes instantly on the suitcase. "So Azziz, you have returned."

Azziz looked at her. She was still almost as beautiful as she had been when his father first brought her to their house. It was after his own mother had died. He was only four years old, but he had been as impressed as the others by her high cheekbones and dark slanting eyes. Esma said she had Mongol blood in her, like the great Chengiz. She was pure Turkish unlike his father who was Kurdish.

Later, when he was grown up, he understood it wasn't just Esma's beauty that had led his father to choose her. Kurdish virgins commanded high bride prices. Turks didn't value their daughters as much. But at the time Azziz had thought Esma was queen-like, and when she had commanded, "Speak Turkish, not that gibberish," he had done his best to comply.

The only problem was that he didn't really know Turkish. Not until he began attending school two years later.

"Does your father know you are back?" Esma said to him when he came back after that summer.

"I am going to America. Dr. Jeem and his wife invited me."

"Invited you," she murmured to herself as if she didn't quite understand.

Azziz waited. He knew what she was doing.

"Is America like a wedding then?" she asked in her high-pitched nasal voice. Esma's voice was the only un-pretty thing about her. "Do you have to be invited? Maybe they'll expect you to bring a gift." She laughed and then turned away from him quickly, bending to pass under the frame of the low, crude doorway.

He watched for a moment as she stood in the sunshine, shaking her finger at the children who were still hanging around, hoping for more treats. He couldn't hear what she was saying, but whatever it was, they cleared off quickly, the small ones running a little, as if they were afraid her words might turn into sharp stones, flying through the air toward their tender little shoulder blades. They knew about her edges. So did her daughters. All of them were careful to stay a good distance away from her. It was only Azziz who had made the mistake of trying to get close. Maybe it was her beauty or maybe it was because he'd missed his own mother so much. People used to laugh about it.

"Azziz is smitten with his stepmother," they remarked.

It was only after his circumcision that he'd finally given up.

"Azziz!"

His half-sister Fawzia was standing in the doorway, silhouetted against the light. "How was the island? Have you become a pasha now?"

She danced toward him into the darkness, her skirts swishing against the carpet. Azziz felt as if he were eight years old again. He had never known how to deal with any of his half-sisters, and Fawzia, the eldest, closest to him in age, was the hardest.

"Is this for me?" Her voice had a crooning quality.

He'd almost forgotten the kerchief he'd taken out of his pocket. He hadn't really decided who it was for, but it didn't matter now. The soft, silky material slid out of his hand as Fawzia grabbed it. He watched as she turned her head this way and that in front of the little mirror, wrapping the cerise and white scarf in different styles. Finally she came over to him, putting her hand on his arm. "Big Brother, I am glad to see you."

He already knew what she wanted.

"You can get another one. You're going to America." Her eyes pleaded with him as she held up the suitcase he'd brought, the one Dr.

Jeem had given him. "I need it for my dresses."

The old lethargy was coming over him. Why not give it to her, a voice inside him asked. She's right. You can get another one. Besides maybe they'll leave you alone if you do this. Maybe they won't mind so much that you're going and they're not.

"No," he said to Fawzia, his voice sounding harsh to his own ears. "I can't give it to you. I need it."

Later when his father returned from the teahouse, Azziz stood as the old man settled himself. His father barely acknowledged his presence. Just a slight nod in Azziz's direction before he faced toward Mecca.

Azziz watched. When his father prayed he threw his whole body into it, beginning with his lips which moved energetically. His face lost its customary sardonic expression and became rapt and whole-hearted-looking. Azziz watched and felt, not for the first time, more than a little envy.

His father loved God. But Azziz could no longer pray the way his father prayed. He didn't know why exactly. He used to pray. Until he came back from the army.

"You're a real soldier now, aren't you," his father had said in a mocking voice while Azziz stood there and said nothing as his father began the *salavat*. Azziz stood there now and waited for his father. When he finished the prayer he stood up slowly, the mask of pain on his face revealing him to be just another old man.

Azziz's heart contracted. Why couldn't his father love him the way fathers were supposed to love their sons? Maybe that was why he had wanted Esma to love him so much.

His father said, "I hear you are going to America."

"Yes, Baba. Dr. Jeem asked me to come there and look after his son."

"Did he?" His father didn't say anything. Just took out his prayer beads and began moving the amber spheres, one by one, along the string. Azziz waited.

Finally his father's thumb stopped on a particular bead. "You have been wanting to go to America for a long time, eh?"

Azziz shook his head. "No, Baba. I didn't want to go to America until Dr. Jeem asked me. You know that, Baba."

"Yes, yes." His father spoke in an impatient tone. Azziz's heart sank.

So nothing would change his father's mind. It didn't matter that he was the only son and the eldest child. Nothing mattered where Azziz was concerned. He had been forced to find his own place in the world.

"Well, America must be a good place. Everyone else wants to go there."

Azziz didn't say anything.

"You go to America." His father waved his hand dismissively. "You will enjoy it there."

Azziz stayed sitting as his father stood up and walked away, mumbling something about Dr. Jeem taking advantage of Azziz. His cheeks burned. He was 24 years old, old enough to have his own land, to bring his own bride, to start his own family. His father could have given him the land to make it possible for him. But instead, Azziz would have to join Dr. Jeem's family and go to America.

On the day of his departure, everyone lined up to say goodbye and tell him what they wanted him to bring them from America.

"And what do you want, Baba?"

The old man laughed. "It is easy to want things from other people.

Easy also to be disappointed. Someday you will learn that." He went back toward the house. Only Fawzia and her younger sister Emine were planning to walk with him out to the road where the bus stopped.

But before his father went inside, he turned around and said, "From Azziz, I want nothing."

After his faint at Mamoulian's, Azziz waited for them to ask how he was or to offer to take him to the doctor. The days passed. Maybe they figured it was nothing. He didn't want to cause trouble so he didn't bring it up. One night he dreamt of the village. It was snowing. Snowing and snowing. Azziz was struggling to walk to the front door of his father's house. Every step he took toward it, the wind pushed him back.

"Baba!" he cried into the wind, but no one heard him. When he awoke in the middle of the night, he was sweating. He got out of bed and went to the window. It hadn't snowed here yet, but Dr. Jeem said it would, soon.

The next morning, Dr. Jeem and Annabel were already gone by the time he had Jacob dressed and eating breakfast.

"Roll," Jacob called, pointing to the mound of flour Azziz had poured out on the counter.

"No rolls yet," Azziz said in the simple English they used together. "Rolls later. Azziz make them."

Jacob was pushing his cereal bowl along the counter. Azziz watched him out of the corner of his eye until it was too late. There was a crash and then soggy Cheerios amid the broken crockery all over the formerly spotless floor.

Azziz felt a headache start.

"More cereal!" Jacob called out.

He poured another bowl, and then squatted down to clean up the mess. Jacob watched with interest.

"Jakey. Look!" Azziz pointed to the clock. "You don't want to be late for school, do you?"

Jacob gave him a cold look.

Only then did Azziz realize. He had spoken in Turkish without even thinking.

He laughed awkwardly and helped the little boy down from his chair and into his outdoor clothes. But there was a rift between them today. Azziz couldn't explain it. Jakey who had always seemed so special to him now seemed petulant, even spoiled. As soon as they reached the school, Jacob ran toward the gate without even a backward glance.

Azziz started walking back to the house. The cold air and the dampness made his joints feel as if he were turning into an old man already. Pulling open the side door he felt the momentary relief at the warm blast of the forced air furnace. But that soon faded. The house felt empty and bare with Annabel's sleek modern furniture. The only old thing was a grandfather clock she'd inherited from her grandfather which she treasured. She liked to show Jacob and Azziz how it worked.

Today even the clock didn't cheer him up. The living room felt empty and alien. The kitchen was where he spent more of his time, he felt better. Pouring the flour out onto the polished granite, he stopped to gaze through the window at the side lawn. When he'd first come here he'd been amazed at how effortlessly all the plants stayed green. But now the cold had set in and the clouds. For more than two weeks there had been nothing but grey skies.

After awhile he went back upstairs. He meant to lie down for twenty minutes, an hour at most. He sank into the soft bed and covered himself with the quilt. The big wooden house creaked and sighed as the wind came up outside.

Azziz shut his eyes and dreamt of his village. He was coming back on the bus. But when he arrived, no one seemed to notice.

"Baba," he said. "I'm home."

His father didn't even give him his usual cold glance. He just went on talking to his family.

"Fawzia," said Azziz in an urgent voice. "I'm here. Back from America."

But Fawzia too was lost in her own little world.

In desperation Azziz went back outside. He went up to the gaggle of children playing. "Remember Uncle Azziz? The one who gave you candy?"

They didn't even look at him.

Azziz felt frightened. What was happening? Suddenly he looked and from far away saw Dr. Jeem coming toward him.

Relief flooded him for a second. Then he realized how far away Dr. Jeem was. He started walking toward him. Walking and walking. But the more he walked, the further away Dr. Jeem seemed.

He wondered how far he'd have to walk to get to him. He felt so tired. All he wanted was to lie down.

He wondered if Dr. Jeem would be disappointed in him, giving up so easily. Dr. Jeem himself rarely gave up.

Azziz gazed across the clearing. Dr. Jeem was standing, shading his eyes against the sun. He thought of shouting, but he knew it was too far.

So instead he lay down on the bare ground. It looked hard and stony but when he sank down, it didn't feel hard at all.

"Azziz!"

Azziz opened his eyes. He peered into the darkness. Why was it so dark?

Then he remembered. He'd been asleep. He started up. Annabel was standing there, watching him, from the doorway. He didn't know how many times his name had been called. Many times maybe.

"Azziz, what is the matter?"

Before he could answer. Jacob rushed in. "Azziz! Azziz! Where were you? My teacher called, but you didn't answer."

So many thoughts went through his mind. The telephone was far away, all the way downstairs. And Jacob's teacher -- he wondered if she was the one with the long honey colored hair -- what had she told Suzanne? He knew he should say he was sorry. He didn't mean to forget about Jacob. But the more Annabel stood there watching him, the harder it was to say anything.

Annabel pressed her lips together. "You should have told us, Azziz," she said in a tight voice.

He heard them going back down the stairs together. Annabel's high heeled tread punctuating Jacob's high-pitched little voice.

A long time later Dr. Jeem came up to see him. Azziz heard his heavy tread coming closer and closer, until suddenly there he was, filling up the doorway.

For a moment they just looked at one another.

Finally Dr. Jeem spoke. "Do you mind if I come in?"

Azziz struggled to sit up.

"No, please. Don't get up for my sake." Dr. Jeem folded himself into the tiny chair at the foot of the bed.

"I need to apologize to you, Azziz. We should have taken you to the doctor before now." He broke off suddenly, and Azziz saw with surprise that beads of moisture had appeared on his boss's high fair forehead. He went on, not in the tone of certainty that Azziz was used to hearing from Dr. Jeem, but in a soft, uncertain voice. "I don't know what happened. How this slipped through the cracks. But I have made the appointment now. We will go tomorrow."

Azziz felt terrible. I am all right, don't worry about me, he wanted to say. But the words stuck in his throat.

The next day the doctor examined him. Tapping him here, squeezing him there. Afterwards the doctor talked to him while Dr. Jeem translated. The doctor asked what had caused his mother to die, and if his father was still alive. Finally he said he could find nothing wrong. To Dr. Jeem he said more — all in English. Azziz heard the word "stress" several times. It was one of the many words he didn't understand. Even to pronounce it, with those three sounds, s,t, and r, together was impossible for him.

On the way home he noticed Dr. Jeem was going a different way.

"Let's get some *lahmajoons*, what do you say?" his employer was asking.

Azziz nodded.

"Azziz, do you like living here?"

The question came suddenly, with no warning. Azziz turned it over in his mind. Like living here?

"It is a nice place. Your house is very comfortable." He paused. "I know I am lucky to be here."

Dr. Jeem turned his eyes away from the windshield. His glance was piercing. "Lucky in what way?"

"Well," Azziz felt put on the spot. "Everyone in Turkey wants to come here."

"But that's not what I'm asking. I'm asking about YOU, Azziz."

Did he want to come here? Azziz felt confused. Why was Dr. Jeem asking him that now?

"Life here is different from life in Turkey. It's difficult, Azziz. Even for me it's difficult, and I've lived almost my whole life in this place."

It was difficult for Dr. Jeem to live in America? The thought struck Azziz with surprise. Dr. Jeem was a professor. Dr. Jeem spoke English.

But Dr. Jeem was continuing. "Life in America is not for everybody."

Azziz didn't say anything. He was thinking about the village. About the slow pace. He was thinking of not ever having to speak English again.

"I don't want to take English classes," he said slowly. "I don't know why." Annabel had been talking to him about going to the local adult school classes. He knew she'd been disappointed when he didn't act interested.

"You don't have to learn English. But you do need to pick up Jacob on time."

Azziz didn't say anything. They hadn't talked about that day again. Now he started to feel bad. He had felt so tired.

"The doctor says I am all right?"

"The doctor isn't sure, but he can't find anything that's wrong with you."

Azziz looked through the window. Ahead in the distance on another block was one of the huge pine trees, the kind he had imagined before coming here. Now he fastened his gaze on it, once more telling himself how lucky he was to be here, how nice Dr. Jeem and Annabel were, how everyone in his village would have wanted to come here.

Dr. Jeem pulled into Mamoulian's parking lot. "Look, Azziz, the choice is yours. You've been here six months. You can go back."

Azziz said, "I will think about it."

That night Azziz had trouble going to sleep. The clock read one, then two and finally three. Azziz closed his eyes. Finally he fell into a dream.

He was back at the dig, the one where he had first met Dr. Jeem. His boss was sitting on one of the old stone thrones. Only this throne wasn't toppled and broken the way the others were.

"Look!" the American said, throwing his arm out toward the endless plain. "Once this all belonged to some great tyrant. But now it belongs to you."

"To me?" Azziz felt confused.

"Yes, to you. Who else, Azziz?"

"It doesn't belong to me. It belongs to the government of Turkey. It belongs to the University of Michigan."

Dr. Jeem gave one of his great laughs. "Don't be silly. Azziz. You're like Jacob. This land is your land."

Azziz stared over the plateau. His land? He had never thought of it that way.

Dr. Jeem was smiling. "Of course it's your land."

Azziz felt puzzled. But before he could figure out what Dr. Jeem meant, the scene shifted. Dr. Jeem had disappeared.

Now he saw his house in the village. He was walking toward it down the road. Would his father be glad to see him this time? Once more hope rose in his chest.

He wondered if his father knew that this land was his land. Maybe if he told him Dr. Jeem had proclaimed it was, his father would give him his share. Or maybe not. He had forgotten to bring his father a gift from America. The thought struck him like a blow. How could he have forgotten? But he had.

In desperation he searched his pockets. There was nothing in them but little bits of grit. Without thinking he put his fingers down into the seam and took some of it out. How strange. He had come all the way back, and yet here were seeds he had bought in America. He put the tiny flat coal black particles into his mouth. Black caraway, Annabel had called them once. But they weren't caraway. Their taste was more delicate than that.

Azziz put his hands back in his pockets. He couldn't believe it. They had filled up with black seeds. Grams and grams of them. He wouldn't ever have to get Annabel to take him to Mamoulian's again. He had enough black seeds to last forever. He could put them on his bread. He could crunch them between his teeth. Their fragrance filled his mind as he sank back into sleep.

The Idle Mill

"Irani shoma?" asked the customs official, fixing Massoud with a hard stare.

Massoud shook his head. "American," he said, pointing to the blue-green passport.

"Amrika'i?" The man repeated doubtfully in Farsi He held the booklet up to his face and studied it, as if he'd never seen such a thing before.

Massoud didn't know whether he should try to make human contact or just stay silent. Who knew what these functionaries of the Shah were up to. One thing he did know was that his place of birth – Kirkuk – was clearly in Iraq. He'd heard that Iranians hated the Iraqis, although whether that included Kurds, he didn't know. In the end he just stood there, as erect as possible. He would not let these people cow him. He was an American citizen now. They couldn't just throw him into one of their prisons.

Just as he was starting to get seriously nervous, the official's interest vanished. "OK," he said, making it sound more like "ochay." Massoud was waved through.

A man with squinty blue eyes and a massive chest came toward him. For a second the Kurdish clothes-- the baggy trousers caught at the ankle, the tight bolero style jacket, and turban-- confused Massoud. Only with the hug, did it fully came back. Homespun wool and acrid Azerbaijani tobacco. Mam Rasheed. His father's brother.

"Welcome! Welcome!" his uncle kept saying, as he put Massoud's luggage into the Land Rover. "It's been too long. How are you?"

But instead of listening to Massoud's account of his last 20 years in America, he began talking about the war. The Americans were arming them and giving them weapons support. The Iraqi government forces were on retreat. Massoud stared through the dusty windshield. In the years since he'd been away both his parents had died. One of his brothers was still back in Iraq. His uncle's words conjured up old longings for the Kurds to finally get their due – to send their children to school in their own language, to not be persecuted for following their own customs, to live without fear. It felt like a letdown not to be able to go home, but instead be here, in neighboring Iran.

They were traveling south, along the edges of a huge salt lake. Massoud had seen it on the map, but he'd never been here before. Occasionally he gazed westward toward the mountains. Beyond them and over the border lay the place where he'd been born. Was his parents' house still standing, or had it been bombed? His uncle hadn't mentioned it.

When they reached the town, his uncle parked the Land Rover in a small cul de sac. They walked over the frozen ground toward an adobe dwelling. A leafless mulberry tree grew in the middle of the courtyard.

The women crowded into the doorway. "Massoud, Massoud," they chanted in unison. "Upon our eyes. Welcome."

He lowered his own eyes, overwhelmed by their solemnity and by the spectacle of their dresses. All those yards and yards of silky satins and glittery brocades fashioned with full bodices, sashed waists, and extravagantly long pointed sleeves. He fought back the feeling of otherness, wondering how Shana would see them. Maybe he should get out his camera and record them right now, before they vanished.

"Come in, come in," they cried. stepping back and making room for him to stoop through the low doorway.

He came in and stood among them. A memory of being a small child, pressed against the skirts of the women, came back to him. He and his mother had stepped out of the sunlight into a small room filled with women-- a wedding, perhaps, or a funeral. The room felt dark after all that sun, darker still when she let go of his hand. He was so short he couldn't see their faces and no longer knew which of the women was her. At first he had wanted to cry out. Only the fear of being shamed had stopped him. But after a moment he had caught his breath and smelled their female smell and been comforted by the rustling of all those yards and yards of gathered fabric.

A sudden irrational urge to kneel down came over him. To go and clasp his arms around someone's skirt and bury his face in the warm folds. Instead, he stepped back, away from them, conscious of how strange he must look. He had not shaved his beard before leaving California, but only trimmed it. Here men wore beards to show piety to Islam.

He looked down at his legs and thought how thin and pitiful they must appear. The men here wore shalwar which were almost as generous with folds as the women's costumes. But he had to stop thinking about how different he looked. It didn't matter how far away you took a plant from the land where it had first taken root and grown. It was still the same plant.

"Friends. Brothers. It's been a long time since I was in Kurdistan." He began to pull at his beard in nervousness until, with an effort, he made himself stop. This was the speech he had imagined giving on the plane. He hadn't been sure if he would actually say all this-- about how glad he was to be back and how much he believed in their Revolution-- but somehow the words just kept coming. He hadn't spoken this many sentences in his own language, his own dialect, in years. At least not in public.

Finally he stopped. One by one the men came over and shook his hand. After that trays of food were brought out. The women disappeared into the kitchen while the men sank to the ground and arranged themselves cross-legged around the edges of the plastic table cloth. His uncle filled his plate with grape leaves, tomatoes, onions, eggplants, and zucchini all stuffed with spiced, meat-flavored rice. There were kibbee, kofteh, chicken, salads and sweets. Pitchers of dew, the national drink of yogurt and water, stood next to green glass bottles of Coca-Cola.

At the end of the feast, his uncle stood up. "Massoud. Come."

Massoud stood up and followed him to a room furnished with nothing but a couple of mattresses and a curtain behind which suitcases and shoes were strewn. A woman appeared and set down a tray with two glasses of tea and a china box containing sugar lumps.

"Please," said Rasheed, gesturing toward the tea. Massoud put the burning liquid to his lips.

"It is good you have come back,' his uncle began. "We need all of our people for this Revolution. Especially the educated ones like you."

Massoud nodded. Yes, he was educated all right.

"We go over the border to fight tomorrow. Are you coming with us'?" Rasheed was watching him.

Massoud felt his face getting warm. Was it the tea that was making him feel this way? It was very strong. He wasn't used to it. In America he had begun drinking herbal teas, the kind of thing people here thought of as medicine.

"I-I don't know that much about fighting," he found himself stuttering.

Rasheed waved his hand. "It is no matter," he said. "No shame. Many of the men who have come back from Europe have never fired a gun. They were never in the army. Like you they were only students. But we teach them. We teach everyone. Guns are not difficult. Especially not for us."

Massoud nodded and then swallowed. A bitter aftertaste lingered on his tongue. The tea had been boiled too tong. The tannin was powerful. He should have taken the sugar.

His uncle leaned forward. "But not everyone is a fighter," he said, in a musing voice. "Not even all Kurds."

Massoud thought of the rivalry between his father and this man. Rasheed was a born fighter, a Pesh Merga all his life. His father had been a scholar. Or wanted to be a scholar. What he'd done for a living was to make shoes. It had been Massoud's job to fulfill his father's dream. But as Massoud well knew the family's admiration had been tinged with other feelings.

Now Rasheed seemed to be letting something go. Perhaps the idea that Massoud would be different. "There are more ways to fight a Revolution than shooting a gun," he said with a tired smile. "I know just the place where we can use you. I'll show you where you'll sleep tonight. We will take you there tomorrow."

The next morning they drove up to a property that looked as if it belonged to a local rich man. Inside the high brick wall was a garden laid out with a concrete pool and dozens of bare branched rose bushes.

"I must go," said Rasheed, looking at the watch which he wore buckled over the cloth of his Kurdish jacket. "But they know who you are. Just go in and speak to the headmistress. Sister Shireen. She is a good woman."

Massoud watched him drive away. The Land Rover careened around the corner. He looked up toward the sloping roof of the school and wondered if he should have come here at all. Last night he awoke in the middle of the night, and remembered a conversation he'd had with Shana.

"Why?" she'd asked him after they'd been over and over the Kurdish struggle and his guilt about not participating in it. She still didn't understand what was driving him to leave his safe existence in America. Now, looking at the school, he wondered if his biggest fear was that the other teachers would regard him as some kind of Johnny-come-lately interloper.

Sister Shireen was smiling at him. She was a big roly poly woman with disorganized, but friendly looking-features. "Kak Massoud!" she exclaimed, her eyeglasses getting skewed in her excitement. "Welcome!" She bustled out from behind her desk and shook his hand. "We've been expecting you!"

He felt a little like a child who had been sent on a mission he wasn't sure he could accomplish. But Sister Shireen seemed to have no doubts about him.

"We are so fortunate, blessed really, to get someone of your qualifications."

For a second he wondered if someone had come in behind him, and

she was talking to that person. He resisted the impulse to look around.
She was talking to him, Massoud, the scholar, with a Ph. D. from an
American university. If anything, he was too qualified. She showed
him to his classroom, introduced him to his pupils, and then abruptly
left. The children sat silent on their benches, staring at him out of huge
long-lashed eyes. Did he once have eyes like that? At the end of the
day in the teachers' break room, one of the other teachers introduced
herself. Zeenay had long braids and high cheekbones.

"How do you like our school, Kak Massoud?" she asked, her mouth
twisting slightly.

He wasn't sure what answer to give. He had so many conflicting
feelings about this place already. "I think it is very fine that the
children are learning in our language," he spoke carefully, not wanting
to give the wrong answer. "When I was growing up I had to learn in
Arabic."

She didn't blink. "The children need to learn Arabic too."

"Of course," he said, and then to cover the silence, asked, "What do
you teach?"

"Mathematics." She lifted her chin.

He studied her. She was very thin with a pretty oval face and
brown braids. When he was twenty he would not have looked twice at
her. But when he was twenty he was on his way to America. America,
he thought, would be full of beautiful blond women.

"Tell me, Brother Massoud," she said with a directness that
surprised him. "Why did you come here?"

No one else had asked him that. They assumed he was here for the
same reason they were. Because he was a Kurd. Because this was
their revolution. Her clear brown-eyed gaze moved back and forth

across his face, searching like spotlights. He felt uncomfortable.

"I came," he said. "Because I wanted to help."

She nodded slightly, as if to say, yes, I know all about that. But the expression on her face asked. Why did you really come? And, what do you really want?

"What's she like?" he asked Ahmed. The two of them were eating dinner. There was only one restaurant in town, or at least only one where Massoud felt safe eating. He glanced nervously around at the other diners who were shoveling in great spoonfuls of rice and washing them down with Coca-Cola.

The waiter set down plates piled with huge mounds of rice with pats of butter and strips of grilled meat laid over them. Ahmed picked up his big spoon and dug in. Massoud studied him. Ahmed was 23. He used to be a physical education teacher at a high school in Baghdad. Now he taught at the refugee school. He was a handsome boy with frank wide set eyes and a ruddy complexion. Massoud didn't know why he wasn't fighting. Maybe because they needed physical education teachers more than they needed

pesh merga. Ahmed, with his open frank face and his enthusiastic ways, was more like an American than anyone else he had met here.

As they ate they talked about what it had been like for Massoud to study in America, and how hard it had been to get university teaching jobs. He broached the subject of Zeenay carefully. He wanted to know more about her, but he didn't want to appear too avid. He remembered the small world of the village where there were no real secrets, and he figured the tiny educated refugee community would be pretty much the same.

"l went to university with Zeenay's brother." Ahmed volunteered.

"Her father's a general you know."

"No, I didn't know."

"Oh yes. He had a commission in the army in Baghdad, before the revolution, of course. The family is an important one."

"She's very smart," Ahmed added.

"Is she?"

"Yes, she finished first in her class at the university. In math."

Massoud caught a man at a nearby table openly staring at the the two of them.

"She's very serious too."

"About what" he asked, one eye on the man who was still watching.

"About everything."

Massoud wasn't sure what that meant. The man at the neighboring table abruptly stood up. He was dressed in cheaply made western style. His eyes met Massoud's once more. He frowned and then walked out. Massoud figured he was part of the Shah's police state, and thought of mentioning this to his new friend, but Ahmed seemed oblivious.

Back at the refugee school, Massoud did his best to teach the students the rudiments of English grammar. In the break room, he made conversation with the other teachers. All of them were friendly toward him. All except Zeenay who continued to regard him with a skeptical look.

The war dragged on. The bombing brought new refugees to Iran. Every few weeks the fighters returned. They brought books and teaching materials, all in the Kurdish language. One week they invited Massoud to go back over the border with them. He wouldn't be able to return to his house, but only go further north. Still he was eager to see what his homeland looked like now. He took his video camera and started filming Pesh Merga on patrol before they asked him to stop for security reasons.

Several weeks afterward, a cease-fire was unexpectedly declared. Ordinary Kurds thought this was a good thing. Now the family and friends they had left behind in Iraq would not be in danger. Only Mam Rasheed and the other leaders knew it was not good for the Kurds. The Shah of Iran had gotten what he wanted, and now it was time for their revolution to stop. The American government, which had promised this would not happen, turned its back on the Kurds. They were sitting on the floor drinking tea. His uncle's back was bent. His voice sounded hoarse as he said to Massoud, "Once again they have used us for their own ends."

Refugee leaders and other highly regarded visitors like Massoud gathered at the house of Zeenay's father. Everyone was milling around, holding glasses of hot tea in their hands as they discussed what to do in the face of this development.

Zeenay's father approached him. "I suppose you will be going back to America soon." He was a handsome man with a broad forehead.

Massoud felt uncomfortable. He mumbled something about how it wasn't right. The Kurds had joined the struggle in order to assert their rights. The Shah had backed them with American guarantees that they would not be double-crossed. Now it had happened.

Zeenay's father waved his hand impatiently "We will find our way," he said. "We are Kurds."

Massoud understood his meaning. The Kurds would survive. The mountains would protect them. Massoud wondered if that could still be true in this late part of the twentieth century.

"But what about Zeenay?" he suddenly heard himself blurt out.

Her father's eyes narrowed. "What about her?" His tone was clipped.

"I can't help everyone in this room," he said slowly. "But I can help one other person besides myself."

Zeenay's father acted as if he hadn't heard.

Massoud forced himself to continue. "Maybe Zeenay could come to America."

The general's grey eyes rested on him, but he still didn't speak.

"I mean, of course, what I mean is. I would like to marry Zeenay." Massoud cursed himself silently. Why had he done it this way? He should have planned it better. He should have gone through the proper channels.

Long seconds passed before the general said, "My daughter has not spoken to me of this."

Massoud felt like an awkward adolescent. Of course the man was right. He stumbled to cover his own mistake. "She has so much promise," he added.

"I must speak with Kak Rasheed," the general finally said, and Massoud's heart leapt.

But in the next breath, Zeenay's father went on. "I don't think it is sensible for these people to go back. The government of Iraq has issued no guarantees."

Massoud felt put in his place. Clearly the general thought he was being selfish. He needed to think about the whole group. The government of Iraq had offered an amnesty. Many people wanted to go back now. They were tired of refugee life. But Mam Rasheed and Zeenay's father knew this to be delusion.

"The Baathists will execute people who have participated in this war," he said.

Massoud did not speak of his own desires again that afternoon. The next day he went to talk to his uncle.

"Simail's daughter? Isn't she somewhat old?" Mam Rasheed's tone was bemused. "We can find you another girl, much prettier, much better."

Massoud understood. Finding a bride was a transaction here. The fact that he himself was nearly 50 would not be seen as a liability at all. Rasheed himself had two wives. The younger one had only been sixteen when he married her.

"She's very smart," he told his uncle. "She deserves to go to America."

"If Zeenay is the one you want," his uncle added, his voice softening. "I will do everything in my power to get her for you."

But it wasn't that simple.

The next time they spoke Rasheed was exasperated. "How can they be so stupid? Don't they realize how lucky they are?"

Massoud felt embarrassed. His uncle was biased. Zeenay's father, on the other hand, could see Massoud more clearly, the way Zeenay saw him. They weren't impressed by his academic degrees or his citizenship. Massoud respected them for that. Still, he wanted her. The more they turned him down, the more determined he was not to go back to California without her. This time he went to her house alone, without Rasheed. Zeenay answered the door.

"I'll get my father," she said. turning away.

"Wait!" he cried out in spite of himself.

He had never seen her in anything but western dress before. She looked mysterious in the long gown of dark gauzy material flecked with silver and over that a short, tight silver brocade vest.

"Zeenay, don't you want to come to America?"

She didn't answer.

He looked directly into her eyes. "If you tell me you don't want to marry me, I will never bother you again. But I must hear it from you," he said. "Not from your father."

She looked at him and then looked away. After a long while she spoke. "All right." she said in a whisper. "I will go to America."

The rest of his stay felt like a dream that unfolded in a series of snapshots. Snap. He and Rasheed were drinking tea with Zeenay and her family. Snap. Zeenay stood in her wedding dress. Zeenay on their wedding night sitting down on the mattress, her dress deflating around her slender body. He didn't see her body that night. They lay down with their clothes on. Later he wondered what had come over him. Why he had been so foolish? It was the custom. You couldn't be truly married without testing the bride's virginity. It was a matter of honor.

But it was too late for that. He was back in America now with his marriage unconsummated. Zeenay's uncles must have thought he was crazy. He shook his head at himself. Well maybe he was. Crazy in love.

Every time the telephone rang, his heart lurched. Maybe her papers were ready. Maybe she would get on the plane today and be in L. A. tomorrow. Waiting immobilized him. He couldn't go look for a job. He couldn't do anything.

Finally the phone rang.

"Allo," said a voice.

He could barely hear what she was saying. The connection

sounded as if it were under water. Suddenly his apartment looked so dingy. All he could think about was the armchair he had gotten from Goodwill. In the Middle East, newlyweds from families like Zeenay's bought brand new velvet-covered furniture.

When she came off the plane, he searched her face for any sign of excitement, but all he saw were the dark circles around her eyes.

"Welcome. Welcome to America," he said.

He had been about to hug her, but she was holding her body like a shield.

"I hope you will be happy here," he said, suddenly overcome with shyness.

Zeenay looked past him.

"We'll just go back to my apartment," he said, taking her bag. "You can sleep as long as you want."

She nodded. He spoke in Kurdish, but the language felt funny on his tongue.

That night a truck went by on Venice Boulevard. He came awake quickly, feeling disoriented. What was he doing in the living room? Then he remembered. He had offered Zeenay the bed by herself this first night. He got up and walked barefoot through the dark apartment. Shadows were moving amidst the lights from the street that shone into the apartment. He opened the door quietly, intending only to check on her breathing. But she was awake in a second.

"Yes?" she asked, sitting up and peering through the darkness.

"I just wanted to make sure that you were all right, that you didn't need anything."

"I am all right," she said softly.

He went closer. "Are you sure?"

"Why are you so worried about me?"

He felt at a loss. He had been trying so hard to be considerate of her feelings. He started to move back toward the door. "If I can get you anything, just let me know."

She pushed the covers back and swung her legs out of the bed. "Why?" she started to say as she stood there facing him.

"Why what?" he asked, feeling confused.

"Why did you marry me?"

He drew in his breath. "Because, because --" He didn't know what to say. He had never heard his own father tell his mother he loved her. It just wasn't done.

"I wanted you to be happy," he finally said.

"Massoud," she said in a firm voice. "I am your wife."

Tears sprang to his eyes. He didn't know why. He had never wanted her to feel obligated to him. She came still closer. She was tall for a Kurdish woman where the most milk and the best food always went to the boys. He was short for a man.

She moved closer and put her hands on his shoulders and. "If I am your wife, you must do to me what men do with their wives. Otherwise there will be shame on both our heads."

He let his breath out as he drew her toward him.

"She's brilliant, maybe even a genius," he told Shana when he ran into her at Safeway the next week.

Shana stared. "I don't understand."

Massoud looked past her at a pile of avocados, their skins pebbled and black. What didn't she understand? That Zeenay was a genius? Or that he had finally gotten married?

"She could do anything. You know she studied mathematics back in Iraq."

Shana was wearing a tube of some hot pink stretchy material that barely covered her breasts. She didn't say anything.

Massoud started to feel guilty. Shana had been nice to him when he was lonely. She hadn't minded his foreignness. But Shana was old. Her skin was beginning to wrinkle and never in a million years would she understand Kurdish customs.

"You must come over one evening and have dinner with us." He took his eyes off the avocados and looked at her bleached blond hair. There was a time when blond hair had meant a lot to him.

Shana was watching him. He knew what she was thinking.

I'm sorry, he wanted to tell her. I didn't plan to marry Zeenay. I only planned to fight in a revolution. But he couldn't say that. He didn't know what he'd planned anymore.

Slowly, other refugees began to arrive. Ahmed, the physical education teacher, came first. They met him at the airport.

Zeenay actually ran toward him. "Ahmed, Ahmed," she called, waving her hand back and forth. Massoud watched. He hadn't seen her this happy since she'd come to America.

When they got back to their apartment, Massoud went to make tea for them. Ahmed and Zeenay stayed in the living room. He hoped Ahmed wouldn't notice how shabby the furniture was or how the rug smelled of mold. He still didn't know if Zeenay had noticed these things.

"How is my family?" he heard her asking Ahmed in the living room. Massoud set the kettle quietly on the burner. He wanted to hear what was being said. Besides mathematics, Zeenay loved only her family. Oh, how she missed them! But Massoud dreaded the day they would all arrive here.

"And what about you?" Ahmed was asking now. "How are you, Zeenay? We were all so happy when Massoud asked you to marry him. You, more than any of us, deserved to have the chance for a new life."

Massoud held his breath. The tea kettle was dancing. He snatched it off the burner. For a second he thought he'd missed her answer. Then he heard Zeenay laugh.

"Me? My life is over," she said in a voice that was carelessly loud.

For a moment he simply froze, as numb as a statue. Then, slowly, he began arranging the glasses on the round brass tray. After that, he poured the steaming liquid. Finally he picked the tray up and carried it, glasses just barely rattling, into the living room.

"Our servant is on holiday," he joked, conscious of how it must look to Ahmed, that he and not Zeenay was waiting on the guest.

"Yes, the servant went back to her village," said Zeenay, catching on immediately.

Ahmed looked from one to the other. "Are there villages in America?"

Zeenay took the tray and began handing around the glasses. Then she jumped up, went to the kitchen, and brought back a box of cookies. "There is everything in America," she said. "Even Kurds." She laughed again.

As they drank their tea, Massoud leaned over and lightly touched Zeenay on her back. It was something no husband would do in Kurdistan-- touch his wife in company. Zeenay looked up quickly, and he was relieved to see a small smile on her face.

"Later I'll show you the film I made in Iraq," he said to Ahmed.

"I've been going around showing it to various groups to raise awareness for our cause."

"So the film turned out all right?" Ahmed wanted to know. "I remember you were so worried about it:"

"It turned out beautifully," said Zeenay while Massoud wondered how long it would be before Ahmed saw that film with American instead of Kurdish eyes.

Later that evening, Massoud kept looking at his wife, willing her to say other things that would show that she really thought well of him, maybe even loved him. But she never repeated her praise of his film, or any other praise.

When they were getting ready for bed, Massoud couldn't help asking her. "Zeenay, don't you want to have children one of these days? Don't you think it would be good?"

Zeenay gave him a long look before she turned out her light and then rolled over to her side of the bed. "Maybe," she told him in a neutral tone of voice. "But first I have to get my degree. You understand, Massoud, that my degree comes first, don't you?"

"Of course," he said.

He lay there in the dark, not knowing if she was awake or asleep, but not daring to speak to her. Tomorrow he would go out and buy the newspaper first thing. There would be no news of the Kurds. The world didn't know or care that their revolution had failed.

The idle mill-- that's what Ahmed had called it.

"The what?" Massoud had been caught off balance. He hadn't forgotten his language. But he didn't think in Kurdish images these days. *Ash betal*. It meant "idle mill," literally translated.

When the revolution had started up people had left their universities in Europe, their jobs in Baghdad, their homes, their neighbors. They had risked everything they had for the dream of an independent Kurdistan. It was like a mill in a village. A mill bought with hard currency. The most expensive piece of equipment a group of peasants would ever buy. You never knew whether in the end the mill would pay for itself. Sometimes the crops failed, and the mill stood idle. It was the worst thing anyone could imagine. All that money spent and no flour to show for it. It meant going without bread for a whole winter.

Massoud listened to the sound of Zeenay breathing. Asleep her face lost the stern look it wore during most of her waking hours. Her mouth looked vulnerable. He wanted to lean over and kiss it, but he refrained because he knew, even though she would tolerate his caresses, her expression would change.

Soon the university would start up. He was afraid of that as he was afraid of everything. Who would she meet there? A young man her own age? One without disappointed eyes? One who had not already failed? His only comfort was in knowing that she was a Kurdish woman raised not the way American girls were raised, but raised to think that marriage would settle her life.

Of course life was never settled. He knew that. You could build yourself a hundred mills, and they could all stand idle. Tomorrow he would buy the newspaper, and he would call the junior colleges, and he would even start thinking of other jobs he could take besides teaching. But for now he was here, beside Zeenay, listening to her breathing. It was a sound he never tired of. Like the sound of the mill humming in the village. An annoying sound, if you thought of it one way. A comforting sound if you thought of how important it was. But

a sound nonetheless. A sound of work being done. Of time going on.
Of the mill not standing idle.

Kharbooza

"You want to buy melon?"

Matt glanced into the long tanned face with its high protruding cheekbones. Above them, set deep into their sockets were the blue eyes of northern Indo-Europeans. He'd seen faces like this before, and melons as well. Even from this distance he could smell their fragrance. Their pebbled skin had no soft spots. At least none he could feel. The price was posted: one dollar a pound.

The melons were large, probably upward of five pounds apiece. He wasn't sure he wanted to spend that much, especially since he probably wouldn't be able to eat it all by himself.

"These are special melons," the man said in a familiar accent. "We call them *kharbooza*."

Matt felt something creep up the back of his neck. Kharbooza sounded too much like the Persian word for melon. He glanced again at the man's face. Surely, he couldn't be Iranian. A lot of the sellers here were from Mexico. Either that or Southeast Asia.

The man pushed the little plastic container of chunks toward Matt. "Here," he said. "You try."

Matt started to say no, and then changed his mind. There were no toothpicks, just a fork stuck into one of the samples. So he picked it up and bit the chunk off carefully The amount of fructose surprised him. His teeth almost ached.

"Very sweet," he said.

The man leaned forward, grasping the edges of the table. "We bring the seeds of these melons from our homeland."

Matt nodded, a little taken aback by the intensity of his gaze.

They'd had melons like these when he'd first arrived in Shahpur. People were selling them on street corners. Persian melons, he'd called them to himself. Melons were his favorite fruit in childhood, and it had seemed like a sign that the Peace Corps should have assigned him to a country where they flourished. So many things had seemed like signs back then. Even the weather. Day after day with no cloud in the sky. God's country was how he'd thought of it.

He studied the melons that were laid out on the crude trestle table and picked up what looked like the smallest one. The man took the fruit and set it carefully on a primitive hanging balance, with a dial instead of a digital liquid crystal display. He turned the dial around so that Matt could see it and understand he was not being cheated. Six and a quarter pounds, it read.

"Six dollars," the man said.

"Four," Matt countered.

The light behind the man's blue eyes crystallized as he took the melon off the scale and laid it gently back on the table with the others.

"You are engineer?" the man asked.

Matt nodded. Here in the heart of Silicon Valley, it was an easy guess.

"And you?" Matt asked.

The man folded his arms across his chest. "I am farmer. But before that I was freedom fighter. In Afghanistan."

Matt knew from experience not to make assumptions. You never knew what side freedom fighters might fight on.

Still he felt obliged to say something. "I wish I had seen your country when I still had the chance."

The man's eyes grew paler. "You were near my country?"

"A long time ago."

"You were in Soviet Union?" the man wanted to know.

Matt shook his head. "Iran."

"Ah, Iran." He leaned forward again, fixing Matt with his stare. "Our melons are better than in Iran."

Matt nodded, "I'm sure they are."

There was a pause while he debated again whether to buy, and then, after thanking the man, he turned and walked away. But as the week progressed, he began to regret his decision. Every time he opened the refrigerator, he found nothing as good as that melon would have tasted.

On Thursday he dreamt he was on a train very much like the train he had taken on his last trip to Tehran. He would never forget that trip. The compartment had been jammed. All men, of course. Even in those days, passengers had been segregated by sex. He had received the expulsion order a week before from the Peace Corps, and his heart had been full of blackness.

In the dream he was back in the second class train compartment, with the same ornate wood trim, the same cracking leather upholstery. The train was clacking across the plateau toward the mountain range separating Azerbaijan from Fars Province. The other passengers were giving him suspicious glances, as if they weren't sure whether he belonged there or not.

He pulled the little cardboard stub out of his pocket with the number of the seat he'd been assigned. The tiny stamped numbers were hard to decipher. But when he looked at the number on the seat arm he saw that they clearly didn't match. He stood up and retrieved his backpack from under the seat. But when he reached to open the door to the corridor so he could find the right seat, one of the men abruptly stood up and with his back against the door, faced Matt with an angry look.

"It's closed," he said in Persian.

"I know," Matt said. "But I need to go out."

The man pursed his lips in a look of disgust and continued to stand there. The other men were glowering. He awoke from this dream sweating.

For a moment he was not sure where he was. Then he saw his face reflected in the mirrored tiles that lined the bedroom wall of the house he'd bought in Palo Alto. He'd been planning to replace them, but this had been put off like everything else in his life that didn't relate to work.

He stood up from the bed and went out into the kitchen where the glass windows showed it was still dark outside. Summer was segueing into fall. He filled a glass with tap water and drank it slowly, staring at himself in the reflective dark of the windows. His face had filled out from the lean visage of a 23 year old. He was a middle-aged man now with a receding hairline and more grey hairs than he cared to notice. His glasses were no longer wire rims the way they had been in Iran. He was clean shaven except for the night's stubble. It was the glasses and the beard that had marked him unmistakably as a foreigner back then. In those pre-Khomeini days, no one but mullahs grew serious beards.

Even with the growing light and the realization he was in another life now — a safe life, full of material comfort — he couldn't shake the clammy fear of the dream. It wasn't even accurate. In the real train ride, the one he had taken all those years ago, he had taken the wrong seat, but the other men hadn't minded, even though it meant there was an extra person taking up space. Why had his dream made them so harsh?

He decided to give his unconscious another chance. Maybe with a little more sleep he'd wake in a more optimistic mood. He went back to bed intending to get up at his usual time of six. He almost always made it into work by seven. But this morning he wasn't even out of bed when the phone rang at 7:15.

"Hello," he said, in a voice still whispery with sleep.

"Hey Matt, I didn't wake you up, did I?" Pam Parker, the group's liaison from Human Resources, sounded bemused.

"As a matter of fact you did."

"Sorry about that." Her tone was flippant rather than genuinely apologetic.

He sucked in his breath. Surely he spent enough time at work without them calling him at home at ungodly hours. But ever since he'd made the mistake of joining management he'd noticed that nothing was ever enough.

"There's someone from MIT – a recent Ph. D. She's out here interviewing with another company. Bob Shelton ran into her and liked what she had to say. He wants you to take her to lunch today."

"So why isn't he the one arranging this?"

"He was, but then he got called out to one of the divisions on some kind of emergency. He asked me to call you."

If it was Bob Shelton's personal request, he didn't have much choice.

As he was driving into work, he realized he had no details on the prospective candidate. But he knew Pam. The whole folder would be on his desk in hard copy when he got in.. Sure enough. He checked the label on the tab first. The hairs rose on the back of his neck when he saw the name. "Sho'leh." Unmistakably Persian. He knew what it meant too. "Flame." Later he would recall the thought — be careful not to get singed.

Matt sat at the table perusing the menu. One of his favorite places, the Grape Leaf, served a mishmash of Middle Eastern food. Armenians owned the place so there were items like dolmeh and lahmajoon as well as felafel and kibbee. Sho'leh was late. By the time she finally breezed in, he was considering leaving.

"Sorry," she said breezily. "I had no idea traffic out here was like this." She was dressed in black pants, black jacket, and a white button down shirt.

He gazed up at her face and then belatedly stood up. Hello, Dr.— " and was horrified to realize he'd momentarily forgotten her name.

She gave a little smile. "Sho'leh."

"Matt." He sank back down into his chair, indicating the extra menu.

"Do you come here often?" she asked.

He nodded.

"Interesting," she mused. "They offer both fessenjoon and felafel."

She had black hair and an aquiline nose. Her eyes were huge in her narrow face and fringed with long, thick lashes. Her fingers were long too and tapered and her wrists narrow. He studied them as she perused the menu. The place was jammed, and the waiter took forever coming back for their order.

"Tell me why you're interested in working for us," he said, thinking this was the logical place to start.

"I thought you were the ones interested in recruiting *me*," she countered.

He felt jarred. Applicants didn't usually lead off like this. "Well," he finally said. "We *are* interested. I mean Bob Shelton was interested." He shut his mouth to avoid inserting his foot any further.

She leaned forward, put her fingertips together and fixed him with a searching look. "I can't tell you a lot, you understand, don't you?"

He felt confused.

"I mean I don't want to be going around giving away my ideas before I am even hired."

Most interviewees didn't talk this way. If they didn't want to give details, they glided over them. They also didn't act as if they were long time industry heavyweights with track records behind them, ready to command whole projects.

"Sure," he said, easily. "Tell me as much as you feel comfortable telling."

The lunchtime crowd trickled out as she sat there talking in the vaguest possible terms of the software platform she would build if given a chance.

She had ordered the grilled swordfish which looked as if it hadn't been much to her liking the way she carefully cut away the skin and other parts she clearly didn't want to eat. At one point she glanced over and eyed his dolmas.

"You like grape leaves?" she asked in her slightly warbling voice.

He nodded. For a second he thought she might ask a personal question, but then she went back to her talk of response times and algorithms. By the end he felt slightly mesmerized. Not by her technical acumen — he couldn't really judge that, being a hardware and not a software guy — but by the graceful way she gesticulated with those expressive hands and the intense way she looked at him.

He wasn't exactly attracted to her — not in the usual way anyway — but he was curious to see what the others in the group would make of her. Besides, if Bob Shelton thought she was hot, who was he to turn her down?

"If you really want a job here, you should come back for a full day. We never hire anyone who hasn't talked with every member of the group."

It was the standard encouragement, but it wasn't offered to everyone. Many people came by and were politely vetted with no further invitations. Clearly it wasn't what she'd expected from the way her lips turned down. He wondered if she was offended. Many people with her credentials expected to get offered jobs right off the bat even at the premier employer in Silicon Valley.

"I know it's cumbersome," he soothed. "But we do it for a reason.

We don't like to lay people off."

She nodded, and a hank of her glossy black hair escaped from the barrette, falling across her face. She ignored it.

"Did you always want to be an engineer?" The question just popped out.

Her eyes widened and then immediately narrowed. She reached down to pick up her napkin which had fallen on the floor."Not really."

"I wouldn't have guessed from reading your resume. BS, MS, and Ph. D. all in electrical engineering. It's pretty impressive."

Her face flushed. "I was always good at math."

"So what did you want to be?"

"I don't know. Maybe an artist. A dancer."

As soon as she said that, he realized that was exactly what she looked like, with her long graceful body and swan-like neck. Even the way she'd moved her feet had reminded him of a dancer. A classical ballerina. She certainly didn't look like an engineer.

He said, "I guess we all had dreams."

"What did you want to be?"

He laughed. "You won't believe this."

She leaned forward. "Tell me."

"A minister."

Her lids flew up, and he gazed again at her lashes. He couldn't believe how luxuriant they were.

"You mean like the Christian Right?"

He laughed. "My grandfather was a Unitarian minister. Not exactly the Christian Right. I admired him a lot."

"My grandfather was a mullah."

"Really!" As soon as the exclamation was out of his mouth, he wanted to call it back. But instead of letting it just rest there for what it was, a statement of his own disbelief, he followed it up with "Is that why you couldn't be a dancer?"

The bold eyebrows knitted together."You know something about mullahs?" Her voice was low and cold.

"Not really," he said quickly, but there was no going back. "I was in Iran, back in the late 70's before uh...." His voice trailed off.

Her gaze became opaque.

He plunged on. "I –uh was in the Peace Corps there. For five months, but --

She cut him off. "You know why I got a Ph. D.?"

He shook his head.

"Because I saw what happened to my father. He was an engineer too."

"What happened to him?" he asked, feeling puzzled.

"My grandfather might have been a mullah, but my father, when he was young, joined the mujahideen. When Khomeini came to power they turned against the mujahideen who had helped him all those years in Paris. My grandfather and my father were already not on speaking terms. We had to flee, but my father couldn't get a job after we moved here. Because of the hostage crisis. Americans saw all Iranians as the enemy. So I decided to stay in school and get so many credentials, the subject of my being Iranian would never come up."

These revelations upended every stereotype Matt had — namely that mullahs were a class apart and their sons didn't become engineers, much less their granddaughters.

Somehow they made it through the rest of lunch. By the time they finished, his stuffed grape leaves and roasted eggplant had turned to roiling acid in his stomach. All he wanted was to lie down, but he had to drive her back, and once he was there he thought it would be bad form to leave.

Pam called the next day."How did it go?" she asked in a voice that lacked her usual pep.

"All right," he said in an equally non-committal tone.

There was a pause. Pam continued, "I think I should let you know. She complained about the interview."

He thought of saying something flippant, but decided Pam would only say he was being defensive.

So instead he said, "What did she say?"

"Only that you were too personal in your questions."

"I got a little side-tracked, I admit, but I think she's kind of touchy. Attitude issues. Maybe it goes with the territory."

"What territory is that?" Pam's tone was frosty.

"Being Iranian."

The silence expanded.

"Have you gone to one of our diversity training seminars?"

Matt laughed. "Don't you remember? I helped you give the one last year."

"Maybe we should do another one. Just for you, specifically on the Middle East."

"Sounds interesting," he said in a bland voice.

By the time he hung up, he felt seriously annoyed. Why had he ever imagined Pam was his friend?

On Saturday he went to the farmers market. The place was overflowing with produce, which was typical for this time of year. On table after table he inspected peaches, plums, apples, tomatoes, cucumbers, squash. He had arrived in northwest Iran at about this same time of year, and he could still recall the myriad booths mushrooming out from the bazaar. It had seemed like a land of plenty then. Even after winter came and the fresh produce had dwindled to stored apples and onions, he still loved the place, the food and the people.

Standing in the midst of this parking lot in Mountain View, Matt recalled how the February air had entered his nostrils like a sharp herb as he rode his motorcycle out to the village that day. The way they had stood out in the cold waiting for the VIP's to show up. The Pahlavi Foundation! It made him angry just to recall the name. Imagine running a country and taking all its oil revenues and then acting as if you were dispensing charity just to provide basic services.

They were lined up there to kiss her hand just for thinking about building a school. She was supposed to be the Shah's mother-in-law. Certainly she was wearing a rare enough fur. A leopard had died so she could look chic. He could still remember the way she had looked at him. With a kind of coquettish expectation in her eyes.

He didn't really know what she wanted. Some kind of validation he supposed. Yes, you're doing great things when, in fact, they were doing nothing. He had started backing away, almost as a visceral response. Certainly he hadn't thought it out. Before he'd realized what he was doing, he had kicked down the pedal on his motorcycle. The engine roared to life like the soul of the dead leopard.

For a week he'd heard nothing. Then Ken, the director in Tehran, had called. "I'm sorry, Matt," he said. "But we can only stay as long as we're wanted; that's the rule."

Matt remembered looking out toward the snow covered mountains and realizing that he would never see the spring there. Never eat mulberries from the tree in the courtyard. Never again talk to the boys in the village.

Now, as he stood in front of the melon seller's table, the man didn't seem to recognize him. "You want to buy melon?" he asked.

"I'll take that one," he said, pointing to his choice.

The man weighed it. "Six fifty," he told Matt.

Matt paid and carried the melon like a baby in his arms, back to his motorcycle where he laid it in the compartment behind the seat.

On Monday morning he brought it to work. At ten o'clock he went over to the little kitchen area, spread out some paper towels, and carved the pale greenish white flesh into approximately one and a half inch cubes. These he put on paper plates with toothpicks stuck into the tops. He set the plates out on his work table with a stack of paper towels next to them. Using a marker and a piece of printer paper, he wrote "PERSIAN MELON" in block letters, and then drew an arrow toward the opening to his cubicle.

The first person to come by was his boss. "How do you know they're Persian?" he asked, as he stood in the opening.

"I got them from an Afghan refugee."

"Yeah?" Bob gave him a curious look, as if knowing the ethnicity of the person you bought produce from was beyond his experience.

Matt held up the plate. "Have some."

Bob reached out gingerly and speared one before putting it in his mouth.

When he finished chewing he said, "That is without a doubt, the sweetest melon I ever tasted."

Matt gestured toward the paper towels. "Take as many as you want."

At noon, he picked up one of the remaining paper towels and wiped the trickles of juice off the table. The one person he'd hoped to see hadn't come by. He'd kept hoping she would, but Human Resources was in another part of the building so she probably hadn't seen it yet.

He picked up his phone.

"Pam Parker," she said in that buttery smooth corporate voice.

"Matt here."

"Oh hi. I was meaning to get back to you."

Matt could hear the hesitation in her voice.

"That's OK," he said. "You like sweet things?"

He heard the intake of breath so he added, "I got some melon here. Bought it at the Farmers Market. I thought you might like a taste before it all disappears."

"Well, I guess I can't miss that, can I?" she asked, her tone warming up.

By the time she walked over, nearly everyone else had gone to lunch. There was one plate left with half a dozen cubes.

"Is this a special occasion?" she asked as she stood in the doorway to his cubicle.

"I met a melon seller from Afghanistan a couple of Saturdays ago. I thought I couldn't eat a whole one, but then I figured out I could – or rather we could."

"Is that right?" she said, eyeing the pieces of melon without picking one up.

Matt said, "I was thinking. Maybe it's time for me to take a leave of absence."

"A leave of absence?" She gave him a surprised glance, which made him feel gratified. So his job hadn't been in jeopardy after all,

"I just realized that I'm not getting any younger." Feeling self-conscious and vulnerable, he added, "Call it a mid-life crisis. But there are some places in my life that I might need to re-visit."

"Like Iran?" she said.

"So you know about my stint there?"

She gave him a funny look. "Of course. Don't you remember? You told me once, back in Berkeley, in the old days. You were really pissed."

"Was I?" Matt felt at a loss. Why had he thought he could keep the parts of his life separate?

She laughed. "You know Matt, I could hardly recognize you when you came to interview at this place. You seemed like a different person."

He wanted to tell her, he felt the same about her, but he felt constrained. So instead he said, "Well I was thinking of going back."

"Maybe you'll run into Sho'leh."

"Why?" he asked, wondering if her wrath would track him even there.

"I called her to set up another interview after the one you guys had, and she called me back and said she had decided to put off taking a job right now. She said she was thinking of picking up lost strands in her life."

Matt felt strange. The world seemed to be getting unbelievably small.

Pam shook her head. "I wish you the best Matt."

"Really?"

"Sure. You're a good man. Just a little lost."

He glanced at her, wondering what she had seen. Pam came from another world too, even though it was just across the bay.

Now she was looking at the melon.

"Have one," he said.

Her hand hovered before she stabbed a piece with a toothpick and popped it into her mouth. A smile spread across her face as she chewed and swallowed.

"I haven't tasted anything this good since I had watermelon on my granny's farm back in Mississippi."

Matt nodded. "Maybe you should go back there."

She laughed. "Hey just 'cause you got unfinished business doesn't mean I got some. No, I'm happy to be right here."

As she walked away, Matt watched her. It was true. She had the walk of a happy person.

He stood up, leaving the last pieces for stragglers. He himself was going out. Not to the cafeteria which would be full of grilled burgers and fries, and the sound of talk from guys who thought the most important thing in life was the next new video game.

The security guard nodded at him as he went past him into the parking lot and across to the grass. It was all dried out this time of year. The rains hadn't started yet. It would be like that in Iran too, if the mullahs hadn't managed to change the weather. The markets would be full of melons, probably for less than a dollar a kilo, considering the competition.

Matt's gaze went further toward the coastal range, which was almost mirage-like this time of year with its pale orange and lavender hues. He tried to imagine getting back on the train and traveling to Shahpur. At first the image was hazy, but as he continued to gaze, he saw it more clearly, and more importantly he smelled it – the late summer corn roasting, the kebabs grilling, the fragrance of ripe melon. It was all back there, God willing, awaiting his return.

END

Acknowledgements

Many thanks to the editors who first published these stories in their original form. Their publications are listed right after the Table of Contents. Very sadly, a number are no longer extant. To the friends and family who proofread and helped me edit the rewritten versions for accuracy, I owe a big debt of gratitude. In particular I would like to thank Susan Kahn, Elyce Melmon, and Millie Moseley for their feedback on early drafts. I want to thank Michael Chyet for giving his expert feedback on the transliteration of the names from Middle Eastern languages. Thanks are also due to Jeff Grote for his painstaking proofreading and for his maintenance of the Pearlnote Press website.

For her marvelous cover, I am grateful to Linda Riddle who helped me conceptualize this compendium and bring it to fruition. To my husband and partner, Phil Wasserstein, thank you for continuing to believe in me and my work.

www.ingramcontent.com/pod-product-compliance
Lightning Source LLC
Chambersburg PA
CBHW030117260626
47156CB00008B/2698